Growing Pains

Daisy Jones

MK

Growing Pains

Dwayne S. Joseph

www.urbanbooks.net

Urban Books, LLC
78 East Industry Court
Deer Park, NY 11729

ISBN 13: 978-1-60162-246-4
ISBN 10: 1-60162-246-5

First Trade Paperback Printing March 2011
Printed in the United States of America

10 9 8 7 6 5 4 3 2 1

Distributed by Kensington Publishing Corp.
Submit Wholesale Orders to:
Kensington Publishing Corp.
C/O Penguin Group (USA) Inc.
Attention: Order Processing
405 Murray Hill Parkway
East Rutherford, NJ 07073-2316
Phone: 1-800-526-0275
Fax: 1-800-227-9604

Acknowledgments

Thanks to God as always for delivering this story to me.

Thanks to my wife and kids keeping me crazy and sane at the same time!

To my friends and family . . . I thank you!

To the readers and book clubs . . . I can't thank you all enough for the support. I am honored to have your support! Here's one to entertain you until the craziness comes in October! I think you will really enjoy this one! I know I did! Keep those e-mails, reviews, and messages on Facebook, and MySpace coming! They mean A LOT!

Portia Cannon . . . thank you very, very much for pushing me on this one! It turned out pretty good, didn't it?

As always . . . to my G-Men! Big Blue!!! All day every day! We've got the NY Giants section going wherever we go! Let's get that Super Bowl!

Much love!

Dwayne S. Joseph
www.facebook.com/dwayne.s.joseph
www.myspace.com/dwaynesjoseph
Djoseph21044@yahoo.com

Growing Pains

Dwayne S. Joseph

1

Jawan was about to lock lips with Janet Jackson.

He was old school. Beyoncé, Rhianna, Ciara, Amerie—they were all sexy, but they weren't women like Janet was. The media would have everyone believe they knew, but they were still learning about control, about how to truly be nasty.

Janet Jackson.

Sexy-ass Ms. Jackson if you nasty.

Jawan was definitely that and he was going to show her. On the beach, as waves crashed rhythmically against jagged rocks, while seagulls soared and called out to them from the sky that was ablaze in orange, red, yellow, and pink hues.

Sunset and the beach—could the setting have been any more romantic?

Janet's classic song "Anytime, Anyplace" whispered softly around them within the ocean-scented breeze. Jawan could only smile at the woman of his dreams. He'd been waiting for this moment for a long time. This time, this place.

He looked at Janet with promised intent in his eyes, and LL'd his lips slowly. Janet gave him her famous I-like-to-make-people-think-I'm-shy smile, and dropped her chin.

You can't fool me, Jawan thought. *I have the* Velvet Rope *CD on my iPod. I know there's a freak there.*

His nature rose beneath his swimming trunks as he traced his index finger up and down Janet's arm. She was wearing a lace-white bikini top, her nipples erect and aching to be released the way Justin Timberlake had set them free. A pink sarong covered her matching thong.

Janet watched Jawan watching her, the glint in her eyes letting Jawan know that she was enjoying his focus. She gave him an intoxicating smile again as he ran his fingers down her cheek to her neck, and then down to the side of her breast. He throbbed again, his manhood wanting reciprocation. Jawan shivered, then held his breath as Janet removed her bikini top, letting free her perfect B-cups, and then unwrapped her sarong and shimmied out of her thong.

"Your turn," she whispered, sitting back, giving him a clear view of the sweetness he and millions of other men yearned for.

Without hesitation, he took off his shorts.

He stared at Janet.

She stared at him.

Waves crashed, seagulls spoke from the heavy air above them.

"I promised I'd be worth the wait," Janet whispered.

She inched toward him slowly. Jawan's heart beat heavily with each sensuous second. The scent of cherries wafted into his nostrils. *So sweet,* he thought. He couldn't wait to kiss, taste her. Janet closed her feline eyes. Puckered her perfectly shaped lips. Seconds passed. Inches decreased. The air became more electric.

And then Grady hopped onto Jawan's stomach.

Jawan opened his eyes and stared at his four-legged companion. "Are you for real?" he asked, his voice tight with irritation.

Grady stared at him.

"Couldn't you have let me have just one kiss?"

Grady stared at him for another few seconds and then meowed.

Jawan groaned and pushed his cat, which was more dog, off of his chest, swung his legs off of the bed, and looked at his alarm clock. Why he bothered setting it, he didn't know. Grady's appearance was clockwork: a half hour before his wake-up time of six o'clock. "Damn Grady . . . that was a long time coming. Why are you hating on me like that?"

Grady meowed again.

"I'm gonna find you a female, and when I do, I swear I'm gonna mess up your flow every time you try to lay it down."

His American shorthair meowed again and then sauntered out of the room.

"Yeah . . . you'll see. I'll make sure she's fine, too. A Siamese with a sweet set of paws," Jawan said, following Grady out of the room and walking down a short corridor to the kitchen.

He'd found Grady scrounging through his garbage cans one morning two years ago. As he did with all strays, Jawan tried shooing the cat away, but unlike most normal cats, Grady didn't run. He just simply took a pause from what he was doing, looked up at Jawan, and then after a meow went on about his business, leaving only after Jawan threw something at him. The rest of the day was as usual until Jawan came home and found Grady rummaging through his garbage cans again. As he had in the morning, Jawan shooed, then threw something at the cat, which disappeared only to return the following morning.

This went on for about a week, before Jawan gave in, went to the store, and purchased a small bag of cat food. He figured that if the cat insisted on being around, he could at least give him real food, thereby eliminating the mess the cat left among the garbage cans. He left bowls of food and water for the cat for about a week, before deciding that since the cat had apparently no intention of leaving him alone, he would take him to the veterinarian to get checked out. A clean bill of health given, and with no signs posted by anyone searching for the shorthair, Jawan took the cat in as his own and named him Grady because of his gray fur.

Grady's company was much welcomed—especially then, as two weeks prior Jawan had just broken up with his girlfriend of three years. Grady was a nice addition to Jawan's apartment, which had fast become one of the loneliest places in all of Queens. Always more dog than cat, Grady craved and loved to give attention. Where Jawan went, Grady followed. The bedroom, the kitchen, the bathroom to take a shit or a shower—no place was off-limits.

Grady was Jawan's pet, child, best friend.

Jawan reached into the cabinet, pulled out a can of Purina, opened it, emptied it into Grady's bowl, gave him fresh water, and then set the bowl down in front of the stove. "Eat up, hater," Jawan said with a smile.

Grady purred and then dove into his food, while Jawan set the hot water to boil for his tea, and slipped three slices of wheat bread into his toaster oven.

As he waited for the bread and water, he looked at Grady and thought about how different life had been just two years ago.

Kim had been around.

Kim, or Kimmie, as he called her. The one he thought was going to be around forever. She'd embarrassed him and broken his heart by betraying his trust. He'd been cheated on once before, but he hadn't considered that a valid heartbreak experience, as he'd only been seventeen at the time. But Kim . . . She'd hurt him, and hurt him badly.

"Who needs her when I've got you, right, Grady-Grade?" he said, removing his toast from the toaster after it dinged.

Grady lifted his head momentarily and then put it back down.

Jawan raised his eyebrows and bit into his toast. A few seconds later, his teakettle whistled.

He fixed himself a cup of Irish Breakfast tea, scarfed down the rest of his toast, and then bent down and pet Grady's head, as the cat was licking his paws.

"Time to get ready, Grady-Grade. It's pop quiz day."

He shut off the kitchen light and went into the bathroom to shave and shower. He didn't close the door until Grady came prancing in behind him.

2

"Mr. White, why you gotta give us a quiz on a Friday?"

Jawan smiled and looked at his most talkative student. "We *gotta* have a pop quiz today, Eduardo, because we *gotta* make sure you stop using the word *gotta*, and use proper English. This is an English class, after all."

"Come on, Mr. White," his class clown said. "You know we don't be usin' no proper English in the streets."

"So are you telling me that after you finish high school, the streets are where you plan to stay?" Jawan asked with a frown. It was a question that should have been answered with a "Hell no!" but he knew all too well, the streets—the very place he'd come from—were where many students ended up when or if they made it out of Franklin K. Lane High.

"That's exactly what he's saying, Mr. White. Eduardo has no goals in life. He wants to be strolling down Jamaica Ave with his boys twenty years from now, with his pants sagging below his ass, broke as a joke."

Eduardo turned to his right and looked across the room at the person who'd answered Jawan's question. "Yo, for real, LaKeisha, why you runnin' your mouth, yo? Especially when I saw your pops rollin' dice down my way with his pants and Tims on two days ago."

LaKeisha nodded as the other students in the room laughed and "ooh'd." The snickering didn't faze her. "My father's a bum, but at least he's a bum who graduated from high school," she said, her voice strong. "Your dumb ass probably won't even make it that far."

Eduardo gave her a hard stare as students laughed at her comeback. "Yo, you ain't special, LaKeisha," he said, stressing the "La." "You act like you gonna be somebody and shit."

"I am going to be somebody," LaKeisha responded, leaning forward on her desk.

Eduardo sucked his teeth. "Man, whateva. You go ahead and get your straight As and shit. You'll still be graduatin' from Lane High. And we all know nobody from Lane makes it anywhere but just past C-Town."

LaKeisha folded her arms across her chest defiantly. "Oh trust me, Eduardo. I'll be making it much farther than the grocery store."

"Yeah, a'ight," Eduardo said, turning back around. "Mr. White, you believe her ass? She be on some pipe dream shit. We all know Jamaica Avenue is like some quicksand. Once you on it, there ain't no gettin' out."

Jawan raised an eyebrow, leaned against the front of his desk, folded his left arm across his chest, and cupped his chin with his right hand. He looked at Eduardo and shook his head. As sad as it was, Eduardo's words were the very same words he'd heard from some of his fellow students when he attended F. K. Lane back in the nineties. As Eduardo said and fully believed, the majority of the high school's graduates never went anywhere past the boundaries along Jamaica Avenue. It was sad really.

Like many of the people he went to school with, Jawan lived around the way also. But his living there was by choice. After high school, he went to college at John J. University, where he earned a degree in business. He moved away from his old neighborhood and went to work in the corporate world as a rep for Citicorp. He wasn't making an exorbitant amount of money, but as far as he was concerned, he was a success, earning more than $50,000 a year. He had a nice apartment in Brooklyn, and took the subway into the city every day.

He'd been one of the lucky ones.

His nephew hadn't been.

He'd only been sixteen when he was gunned down after an argument with another young kid from the same block he lived on. The argument had been over a girl—neither one's girlfriend.

The death of his nephew hit Jawan hard. He'd grown up in the days when fists were used to settle disagreements. You had beef, you settled it man to man, while everyone stood around and watched. There was a winner and a loser. There was no retaliating. You manned up. If you lost, you took the loss and kept it moving. But over the years times changed. Fathers were either locked up or completely absent, and mothers, if they weren't strung out, had to work two or, sometimes, three jobs just to keep a roof over their heads and put food on the table. This of course left their kids alone to basically raise themselves. Some, if they were lucky, had their grandparents there, but the grandparents could only do so much.

Jawan's nephew was a product of that broken-down environment. His father was in jail for murdering a man during a carjacking. He actually hadn't seen his son since his son was five years old. His mother worked two jobs, and when the income from both jobs wasn't enough, she began stripping and selling her body. Jawan's nephew had no one to guide him, and, as a result, the streets and the wrong people in the streets helped to raise him. No one ever taught him how and when to walk away.

Jawan hadn't been to blame for what had happened to him, but he did feel responsible. Work kept him busy and he never had the time to keep tabs on his only nephew. After he died, Jawan quit his job at Citibank, moved in with his sister, who was dying slowly from depression, went back to school to get his teaching degree, and worked part-time to maintain. He couldn't do it for his nephew, but he wanted to make a difference in another youth's life.

After earning his degree, he walked into F. K. Lane and applied for a job teaching eleventh grade English. Five years had now passed, and, despite the city's shortcomings in providing the necessary materials and tools to help students excel and succeed, and the struggles with parents to get them involved in their kids' lives, Jawan's determination to make a difference hadn't wavered.

He looked at Eduardo. "Why does her wanting to leave the neighborhood behind have to be a pipe dream?"

"'Cuz . . ." Eduardo paused, looking for the words. "It just is, son. I don't know nobody who's made it out of here. Ain't no one in my family ever made it. No one in my girls' families. My boys' families. Nobody, son."

"I made it out of here," Jawan said, his voice even.

Eduardo looked at his teacher. "You grew up here?"

Jawan nodded. "Over on Grant Street."

"Word?" another student, DeSean Garrett, said.

"I used to live at the end of the block," Jawan said, smiling. "I graduated from here in '96."

"So then what, you went to college?" Eduardo asked.

Jawan shook his head up and down. "I did. I got my degree in business and then went to work for Citibank."

"So if you made it out, then what are you doing here?" DeSean asked.

Jawan clenched his jaw for a moment and looked around the room at the students in his class, as they watched him with attentive eyes, waiting for his answer.

So young, he thought, looking at them. Young and desperately needing people to believe in them, to show them that anything was possible. That if they put their hearts and souls into it, nothing and no one could stop them from achieving their dreams.

His eyes scanned over a framed photograph of President Barack Obama on the wall behind them. He'd had his students watch the inauguration of the forty-fourth president. He wanted them to see what hope and persistence could deliver. It was a day Jawan would never forget and one he never thought he'd ever see.

"I lost someone very close to me," he said, looking from DeSean to Eduardo and then to LaKeisha. "My nephew. He was sixteen and, just like you, Eduardo, he believed the streets was all there was. He was shot and killed senselessly. I came back to Lane High because I wanted to make a difference. I wanted to try to keep other kids from winding up like my nephew did."

The classroom was silent as Jawan took a breath and let it out slowly.

After a few seconds, Eduardo said, "My cousin was killed for his silver chain around his neck."

"My older brother's doin' ten years for killing his ex," DeSean chimed in.

"My best friend's brother was shot. He didn't die, but he's paralyzed from the waist down," LaKeisha added. "He was trying to be down with the Latin Kings."

Jawan sighed. That was the problem with inner-city kids. All of their stories sounded the same. "Being a graduate of F. K. Lane doesn't define you guys. And, contrary to popular belief, you can escape from Jamaica Avenue."

"Escape to what though?" Eduardo asked.

Jawan looked at him. "To your dreams," he said. "You just have to want whatever it is that you want bad enough, and go after it with absolute belief that no one and nothing is going to stand in your way. See. Believe. And attain. You have to see what you want. Believe you can have it when you do. And then just go after it and attain it. See. Believe. And attain."

"Preach, Mr. White," LaKeisha said, garnering laughter from the students.

Jawan shook his head and smiled as sadness simmered inside of him. Despite his encouraging words, and no matter how hard he worked to keep it from happening, he knew that only a small majority of the students sitting before him were going to move on to life beyond Jamaica Avenue. It was a sad statistic that just seemed impossible to overcome. But Jawan would keep trying to do just that.

"OK," he said, reaching behind him and grabbing a stack of papers from the corner of the desk. "It's quiz time. Books on the floor."

A collective groan rang throughout the room as the students closed their books and placed them beneath their chairs.

"I know," Jawan said, walking around the room and placing the pop quizzes face down on their desks. "I'm losing cool points for doing this to you."

"You're losing mad cool points," Eduardo said as his teacher walked by him.

Jawan let out an exaggerated breath. "I'll have to find a way to deal with that," he said. "But even if I can't, at least you'll all have one hundred percents to show for it, because I know that everyone has been paying attention in class and studying extra hard at home at night. Right, DeSean?"

DeSean looked up at him as he paused by his desk. "Right, Mr. White," he said with little enthusiasm.

Jawan gave him a nod, then finished passing out the rest of the papers, and went back to his desk. He sat down, folded his arms across his chest, and said, "I want all papers on my desk in fifteen minutes, ladies and gentlemen."

Another collective groan rippled through, and then there was nothing but silence and the sound of papers rustling.

Ten minutes into the allotted quiz time, one of his best students approached the desk and laid down his quiz.

Jawan looked up from a crossword puzzle he was working on. "Done already, Brian?"

Brian Moore said, "Yeah."

Jawan nodded and then caught a glimpse of some bruises on Brian's knuckles. Quietly, he said, "Stick around after class, OK?"

Brian gave a nod and walked back to his desk.

Jawan watched Brian walk away, and shook his head. His story was similar to many of the kids in the high school, but unlike many of the knuckleheads who had brains and the ability to succeed but didn't use them, Brian did use his. He, along with LaKeisha, was an A student in the class. Although he never said much during class, Brian paid attention and put the time in at home. Acing tests, surprise or otherwise, was never a problem for him.

Staying out of trouble was.

Jawan had always seen something different in Brian's eyes. A seriousness and maturity level that many of the other kids didn't seem to possess. In a lot of ways, Brian reminded Jawan of the nephew he'd lost. Without being too overbearing, he'd made it his personal mission to guide, or at least try to guide, Brian.

Twenty minutes later, after all papers were turned in, the students rushed out of the class to enjoy their weekends. As had been requested of him, Brian remained behind in his seat.

Jawan finished running red marker over one of the quizzes, and then neatened the stack of papers and placed them in his briefcase. He stood up and walked over to where Brian sat. "You got an A on the quiz," he said, looking down at his student, who was fiddling with his pencil.

Brian shrugged. "Yeah, I know."

Jawan smiled. Brian wasn't being smug. A's were just what he'd expected. "So what's up with the bruised knuckles?" he asked.

Brian looked down at his right hand, flexed it a couple of times, and then shrugged his top lip. "Just got into a li'l somethin' last night."

Jawan looked at him disapprovingly. "A li'l somethin', huh?"

"Yeah," Brian said. "Just a li'l."

Jawan frowned. "Your mom know about this li'l somethin'?"

Brian shook his head. "Nah. Wasn't nothin' for her to really know."

Jawan nodded. "Brian, you know, you're too smart to keep getting into these li'l somethin's all the time."

"I was just defending myself."

"Isn't that what you said last time?"

Brian shrugged with his upper lip again, but didn't say anything.

"You know, if you stop hanging out with the wrong crowd, you wouldn't have to defend yourself all the time."

Brian exhaled. "It's not that easy, Mr. White."

"Of course it is, Brian. You're a straight-A student with a very bright path ahead of you. Remember what I said earlier? See. Believe. And attain."

Brian shook his head. "That sounds good, but, unfortunately for me, I don't see anything."

"Well, if you stop hanging with people who do nothing but waste your time, maybe you would see something."

"Those are my boys, Mr. White. I've known them since kindergarten."

"Well, you know what, Brian? For them being your boys, you sure as hell don't have a lot in common with them. Because as far as I know, you're the only one who gives a damn about being in school."

Brian slumped back in his chair and folded his arms across his chest. "They don't have ideal situations at home."

"I guess you do, huh?"

Brian clenched his jaw.

Jawan frowned. "Look, Brian, I'm all for maintaining friendships, but whether you want to admit it or not, you're not like your boys. You may not know what it is that you want out of life, but I think you're destined for something that will take you far away from Jamaica Avenue, and I think you know it too. Kids like you and LaKeisha are special. You don't have to know what you want to do just yet, but if you just give yourself a chance, your path will reveal itself, and then you'll be on your way to believing and attaining.

"But if you continue to hang with your boys just because you've known them since kindergarten . . ." Jawan paused, turned his palms up toward the ceiling, and shrugged. "You have a hard or easy decision to make, Brian. You can do the easy thing and continue hanging with your boys and getting into li'l somethin's while life and opportunities pass you by, or you can make the hard decision by letting them drift to the side, while you make the most out of all life has to offer. Personally, I think that's the easy decision to make."

Jawan raised his eyebrows and shrugged again. "Anyway . . ." He moved away and went back to his desk. He wanted to get his message across, but he didn't want to over-do it. He had a good relationship with Brian and he wanted it to remain that way. He grabbed his briefcase. "Are you going to the dance tomorrow night?"

Brian rose from his desk and slung his book bag over his shoulder. "Yeah, probably."

"Are you going with Carla?"

Brian shrugged. "I don't know. Maybe."

"Well, I'll see you there."

Brian's eyes widened. "You're goin'?"

"Yeah. Principal Myers twisted my arm into being a chaperone. I kind of had no choice."

Brian laughed. "Unfortunately, my mom will be there too."

"Oh yeah? She's chaperoning?"

"Yeah."

Jawan nodded. "It'll be nice to see your mother again."

Brian looked at him and raised an eyebrow. "OK," he said slowly. "Just don't be talkin' to her too long. It's bad enough she'll be there. The last thing I want is for people to see you talkin' to her like there's some conference goin' on about me."

Jawan laughed. "OK. I promise to just make it a hi-bye kind of thing."

Brian nodded. "That's cool."

"All right, so I'll see you tomorrow. Just do me a favor, Brian. Try not getting into any li'l something's tonight, OK?"

Brian said, "Sure," and then walked out of the classroom.

Jawan frowned.

Too much potential, he thought.

He hoisted his briefcase off of his desk and walked out of the room. Tomorrow, at the dance, he'd make sure to have a talk with Brian's mother about the li'l somethin's he'd been getting into. He couldn't save his nephew, but he was damn sure going to try to save Brian Moore, whether he wanted him to or not.

3

"Yo, Tyrel. Wait up, son!"

Tyrel Gardner stopped walking and turned around. He nodded to Brian and continued his conversation into his cell phone. "Yeah, a'ight, nigga, we'll be there. But don't be fuckin' late like last time. Y'all almost got a nigga thrown in jail for that shit. A'ight, holla." He hung up the phone and then extended his hand to meet Brian's for a pound. "What up, son. I didn't think you were comin'."

"My bad, yo. I had to hang back after class to talk to Mr. White about some shit."

"A'ight. I don't like a lot of the teachers, but he's a cool-ass dude."

"Yeah, he's a'ight," Brian replied with a nod, downplaying the level of respect he actually had for his teacher. Other than his boys, his teacher was one of the realest people he knew, and although Brian didn't say or show it, he appreciated the fact that his teacher tried diligently to keep his head twisted on straight.

"He's one of the only ma'fuckas in Lane who actually gives a fuck about us."

"Us?" Brian said with a smirk. "Since when did *your* ass become a student?"

"Nigga, please. My name be on the roster."

Brian laughed. "Nigga, you hardly go to school. I'm surprised they didn't take your name off that shit."

"They keep my name there for the celebrity status."

"Whateva, nigga."

Tyrel gave Brian a friendly, but rough, shove. "My boy, Mike, said he be seeing Mr. White down at the gym, hittin' the punching bag and sparrin' and shit. He said he's not a nigga to be slept on."

Brian nodded and lit up a Newport. "Yeah, I heard that too," he said, taking a drag on the cancer stick and blowing out a long stream. Smoking was a habit he'd picked up in seventh grade. His mother had no clue he smoked, and if she saw him, he had no doubt she'd kill him.

Tyrel took out his own cigarette from his pack—Marlboro—lit one, held it between his thumb and index finger, and took a deep drag. He smoked and held the cigarette the same way he did a joint. "Mike said that nigga got family around here."

Brian took another puff on his Newport. "Yeah. He grew up on Grant somewhere."

"Word?"

"Yeah. He graduated from Lane back in '96," Brian said, repeating the details his teacher had shared earlier.

Tyrel took another long drag, held the cancerous air in, and then blew it out slowly. "Shit, I know when my ass graduate I ain't never stepping back in that ma'fuckin' school."

"Yo, son," Brian said, laughing. "How you gonna graduate when you don't go to school?"

Tyrel laughed too. "Fuck you, nigga. I be at that school."

"Detention don't count, son."

Both guys laughed.

"Yo, where's Will at?" Brian asked after another pull on his Newport.

Tyrel blew out a cloud of smoke. "That nigga's over at Shauntel's crib."

"Word?"

"Yeah. He think 'cuz her moms ain't home, he's gonna get to hit it. You know he been tryin' hard for that."

Brian shook his head. "That nigga ain't gonna hit a damn thing. Man, Shauntel is tighter than my mom with dough. She don't be givin' up shit."

"Yo, I told him that already. But you know Will—he a hardheaded ma'fucka."

"Yeah."

Tyrel and Brian continued down Jamaica Avenue toward Cross Bay Boulevard. A wicked breeze whipped around them, forcing Brian to zip up his New York Giants bomber jacket. Tyrel, always wanting to show how much of a man he was, kept his bomber open.

"Yo, what's up for tonight?" Brian asked. It was Friday and he was ready to get into something. Preferably Carla, but she had said something to him earlier about maybe having to go to church with her mother. He hoped she wouldn't have to, because it had been a week since they'd last had sex.

"Yo, it's on, kid," Tyrel said, throwing his smoked butt to the ground and lighting another.

"What's on?"

"Remember what we was talkin' about the other night by Will's crib?"

Brian thought hard for a long moment. "Shit, nigga. We were high as fuck. We talked about a lot of shit."

"Man. We was talkin' about rippin' off that Laundromat?"

"Oh yeah," Brian said, nodding. "You wanna do that shit tonight?" He stopped walking and faced his boy, who he'd known since elementary school, and who his mother couldn't stand. He remembered the conversation they'd had about pulling off the robbery, but secretly he was hoping Tyrel wasn't serious about it.

About six months ago, he, Tyrel, and Will had formed a three-man cartel, giving themselves the moniker of

The Notorious Three. Late at night or early mornings, they hit corner stores, pizza shops, and other small stores along Jamaica Avenue and on Rockaway Boulevard. Although being part of the cartel was exciting, and had been good for keeping money in his pockets and expensive clothing on his back, Brian had been looking to get out of it. As much as he tried to deny it, his teacher's words and persistence to make him listen had been having an effect on him. As each day passed, he found himself thinking more and more about his future. He'd told Mr. White that he didn't know what he wanted to do with his life, but that had been a lie. He knew exactly what he wanted to do. The talk about robbing the Laundromat was just that to him—talk. The Laundromat was a much bigger target than anything they'd hit.

"Yeah," Tyrel answered. "Tonight is the night. Kid, I got the whole plan organized and ready to go. Will is down, of course. And Big Mike got us a couple of .45s." Tyrel looked at Brian with hard eyes, who looked back at him with surprise in his. "Don't tell me you're not down, son. I know you ain't backin' out on your boys."

Brian leaned back against a building wall, and waited to speak while the J train passed by on the overhead tracks above him. As it rumbled by, he stared back at his friend. They'd met in kindergarten and had been running buddies ever since. Though they were the same age, Tyrel was like an older brother Brian never had. Tyrel was the ringleader of the clique. He was also the biggest of the three. When he wasn't off somewhere getting into trouble, his spare time was spent working out. Tyrel looked like a miniature Incredible Hulk, with a wide nose, beady eyes, a bald dome, and the most scarred-up hands Brian had ever seen.

Besides being the biggest, Tyrel was also the most violent of the three. His disregard for authority had

had him locked up in the juvenile penitentiary more times than Brian could remember. Fortunately, he was still a minor. But that would change by the beginning of the coming spring. Raised by only his grandparents, as his mother had given him up, Tyrel came and went as he pleased. He also attended school whenever he felt the need, which was usually only to collect some money. The teachers never bothered with him because they were simply too scared to say anything.

His crooked mind constantly working, Tyrel was always coming up with some moneymaking scheme, or some small-time heist to pull in fast money. No one had had Brian's back more than Tyrel had. When an alibi was needed, he was there to provide one. When his funds were short, Tyrel had money to lend. Brian knew that if the time ever came, Tyrel would lay his life on the line for their friendship. Brian had to respect that. You weren't a man if you didn't.

When the J train's loud rumbling faded away, Brian took a long, final pull on the Newport and then threw the butt to the ground. "Yo, kid, you know I ain't backin' out on y'all. I'm sayin' though, the Laundromat's a big spot."

"So what? You scared, nigga?"

Brian shook his head. "Nah, I ain't scared. I'm just sayin' we been doing fine with what we been doin'."

"Those other spots are small time, son," Tyrel said. "It's time for us to step our game up."

"Why we gotta have the .45s? We ain't never needed them before."

"Chill, son," Tyrel said. "We ain't gonna use them."

"Man, I ain't tryin' to be all Scarface and shit," Brian contested.

His hands in the air, Tyrel said, "Yo, son, you soundin' like a bitch right about now."

"Whateva, man. All I'm sayin' is we never took no

guns before. What's wrong with the blades we been using?"

"Yo, I told you it's time to raise the stakes, nigga. Stop bitchin' out on me. Them shits won't even be loaded. We're just gonna have them as a scare tactic. You know how smooth shit always goes for us. All we gotta do is like what we talked about. Roll in, flash them shits, grab the money, and then be out. Kid, the whole thing should take about five minutes, tops. Then we'll roll to Shawn's joint over on Flatbush. You know all the bitches be at his shit. Plus, I heard Jay-Z might be there too."

Brian lit another cigarette and took a long pull. Shawn Colbert had graduated the previous year and was now working for Bad Boy Records as a DJ/producer-in-training. Shawn always threw hot parties back in the day, but now that he'd moved up, the level of the jams he threw had too. Normally, Brian would be amped to hit Shawn's parties, and the thought of missing it didn't exist. But his mind had been occupied by Carla lately, pushing Shawn's party, despite Jay-Z's possible appearance, to the back of his mind. He was supposed to hook up with her until her mom had said something about them having to go to church. As off the hook as the party would be, Brian was hoping that the church plans would be cancelled. He was feeling Carla more than he would ever admit to his boys. He said, "Five minutes, huh?"

"Five minutes, son. In and out and be on our way."

"How much we talkin'?"

"Nigga, you know how those fuckin' Indian ma'fuckas be rakin' in the dough in there. I'd say we roll outta there with at least a G and a half."

"Split four ways?"

"Nah. Split three."

"And what about Big Mike?"

"Shit, that nigga owes me for keepin' my mouth shut when he was locked up and got ass-fucked by some niggas up in Rikers."

"Word? How you found out about that shit?"

"My uncle was locked up at the same time."

"Damn. Your uncle swings that way?"

"Yo, son, my uncle ain't no fuckin' homo. He was just locked up there. He remembered Big Mike from pictures up in my mom's crib. Son, Big Mike'll do whatever the fuck I tell him to do. It's either that or the word is out. You the only nigga I told about that, because I trust you. I would tell Will, but he got a big-ass mouth sometimes."

"No doubt."

"So you down?"

"I already told you I was down, man. I ain't never backed out before. Why would I now? Shit, I just want to do it and then roll. I'm tryin' to hook up with Carla tonight."

"You be hittin' that ass hard, huh?"

"Of course, son. You know I got it like that. I ain't no Will, that's for damn sure."

"I feel sorry for that nigga sometimes."

The two friends laughed, and then Tyrel's stomach grumbled. "Yo, let's get some pizza, son. I'm hungry as a ma'fucka."

Brian nodded. "A'ight. But I'ma have to skip going to Cross Bay and get home after that. I got some shit to do before later tonight."

"That's cool. Just make sure you show up at Will's later."

"I told you I ain't backin' out, son."

Tyrel looked at Brian hard. Brian returned his friend's gaze with an equally stoic stare. He would show up as he promised he would, but inside he'd be hoping for a change in plans.

Tyrel was right: things did always go smoothly for them. But despite the fluidity of the heists they'd pulled, Brian had a nagging feeling that a rough patch was coming, and that they needed to quit while they were ahead, before something went horribly wrong.

4

After eating the pizza, Tyrel went back to his grandmother's house while Brian went home. His mother had left him a list of things she wanted him to take care of for the weekend. To save himself the drama and headache, he wanted to get a good head start on the list and knock out as many things as he could. That would keep her off of his back—at least a little bit.

His mother had sacrificed a lot to provide a home and stable life for him, and for that, Brian would forever be grateful. Her presence in his life was one of the reasons he did well in school. Quite simply, she wouldn't allow him to fail. But she could only be on him so much, and because she spent the majority of her days going between two jobs, she wasn't able to police his extracurricular activities. She had no clue about the li'l somethin's he got into, or the crimes he committed with Tyrel and Will, and if she were to find out, Brian knew that she'd, first, be devastated, and then, second, flip out and go ballistic.

Although he still considered her to be his truest best friend, his relationship with his mother had become strained as he'd grown closer to adulthood. To her, he would always be that little boy she used to take to the park and push on the swing. Brian understood this, but had trouble accepting it nonetheless.

After completing at least half of the items on the list—cleaning the bathroom and his room, doing the dishes in the sink and the vacuuming (which he knew he would have to do again before the weekend was out anyway)—Brian lay down for a quick nap, his mind on Carla.

Just as Will was stuck on Shauntel, Brian was completely into Carla Quinones. However, unlike his boy, who just couldn't get past second base no matter how hard he tried, Brian had hit home runs with Carla many times.

Carla was the half Brian seemed to need to complete him. With his mother being from Trinidad, Brian grew up deeply rooted in his Caribbean culture. The air with which he carried himself was different, and although the way he talked and expressed himself was similar to his boys, there was still something that had always been different about him. A pride that only those of Caribbean background could fully understand. Brian loved his heritage. He loved the food, and the rhythmic rise and tones in the accent of his mother and relatives (an accent that he carried traces of) that misinformed people wrongly confused with being Jamaican.

But the music.

While he did enjoy soca and chutney music, Brian had always had more of a connection with Latin music, especially salsa, and now reggaeton. He could go to a Caribbean party and wine up on someone all night long, but the music still didn't send chills through him the way the salsa did.

He'd often wondered why that had been the case, especially since his mother didn't listen to it, save for the few commercial artists everyone enjoyed: Marc Anthony, some Shakira, and a little Ricky Martin, whom Brian just couldn't get into. The only thing Brian could surmise was that his love had come from the little bit of exposure he'd gotten as cars passed by in his neighborhood, or from some of the homes playing it. Or maybe the love ran deeper than that. Maybe the love had come from the Venezuelan father he'd never known.

Salsa, reggaeton, and merengue when he was at a club—music that moved him.

Music that moved Carla less.

Born from both a Dominican mother and father, Carla's backstory was similar to Brian's. She too had grown embedded in her culture. She loved everything about being a *Dominicana,* but just as Brian had love for music from another culture, so did she.

Soca, chutney, reggae.

These were the sounds that moved her, and ran like fire through her veins.

Before Carla, Brian had dated only American black females. Things were always great with them, or as great as it could have been for his adolescent age, but the one barrier that remained a constant problem was his love for music. The females could deal with reggae and some of the soca, but they could never get into the Latin rhythm.

And then Carla came along.

He'd been into her since the tenth grade, but had never gone after her. But during his junior year, he found out that her favorite music was soca—something he'd discovered during ninth period study hall, as he eavesdropped on her conversation with her girlfriend about her then-boyfriend's reluctance to even try to dance or listen to it—Brian decided right then and there that she had to be his.

Very smoothly, he began a conversation with her about music, and before the period had ended, he had her phone number. Two weeks later, Carla broke up with her boyfriend. And two weeks after that, Brian had what he'd wanted.

Carla did it for him. He hadn't admitted it to anyone, but he loved her. He didn't know what was going to happen when they finished high school next year, but if he had his way, they were going to leave Jamaica Avenue behind together.

Carla.

It was cliché, but she just seemed to complete him. The nagging feeling that something bad was coming stirred deep within the pit of his stomach as he lay in his bed, and before drifting off to sleep, he resigned himself to hitting the Laundromat with his boys. But this would have to be his last job with them, because he didn't want anything happening to take him away from her.

Mr. White had talked to him about seeing, believing, and attaining. Maybe it was time to share what it was that he saw in his future.

"My nigga! What up, son. We was just wonderin' where you was at."

Brian looked at his boy, Will, and gave him a pound. At twenty going on forty, Will was the third and oldest member of the crew. He had been in sixth grade when Tyrel and Brian were in third. They met Will as he was being beaten on by a boy-girl tandem behind the school. The girl, upset at Will for touching her where he shouldn't have, had called on her brother to help her defend her honor. Because they felt sorry for the short, overweight kid with glasses, Tyrel and Brian got Will out of that jam by doing a little beating of their own. Will had been down with them since then.

With his doughboy frame, Will was the weakest of the three, but he had an ugly side to him that, when unleashed, could be very nasty. Like Tyrel and Brian, he had no male presence in his life, but unlike them, his father had been around in his life until he passed away from lung cancer when he was only thirteen. Unable to deal with the loss of her husband, his mother sought heroin to sooth her pain, and became addicted. No longer living at home, his mother could often be seen roaming around in the seedier parts of the neighborhood, doing whatever she had to, to score a hit.

Thrust into becoming a parent for his younger brother and sister at home, Will did whatever he had to do to hold things down. His day job was delivering soda and beer to the corner stores along Jamaica Avenue and Cross Bay Boulevard every day, but the money he made was minimal at best. He wanted more, but he'd had to drop out of school during his sophomore year, so without his diploma, his options were limited. When Tyrel first brought up the idea of forming the three-man clique, Will, desperate for just having the chance of getting more money, didn't hesitate.

"My bad," Brian said, stepping past him. "I had some shit to do for my mom and then I crashed." He walked into the living room, where Tyrel and Heavy D look–alike, Big Mike, were sitting on the couch, playing *Madden NFL* on the Xbox 360.

Brian looked at Big Mike and thought about the secret Tyrel had revealed to him. Although what had happened to him had been no laughing matter, Brian still had to stifle a laugh.

Tyrel looked up at him. "You awake now, right, son?"

Brian nodded. "I'm awake."

Tyrel dropped his controller and stood up. "A'ight, cool. Let's formulate this shit then."

"Yo, son, what about the game?" Big Mike asked.

Tyrel looked down at him. "Nigga, I'm up by thirty-five points. What game?" He walked away from Big Mike, who frowned, and, without a reply, ended the game and went back to the main menu to start a new one against the computer.

Will and Brian followed Tyrel to Will's bedroom, where his brother and sister were boxing on the Nintendo Wii.

"Yo, you two gotta be out," Will said to his siblings.

His eleven-year-old brother groaned. “Aw, man. Come on, Will. I’m kickin’ her ass right now.”

“Whatever, Marcus,” Will’s ten-year-old sister said. “I was lettin’ you win ’cause I kicked your ass in all our other fights.”

Will, Tyrel, and Brian laughed as Marcus’s lips got tight.

Will said to Marcus, “I told your ass to practice before you stepped to her again.”

Marcus sucked his teeth. “Man, she be cheatin’.”

“Whatever, Marcus,” his sister said, curling her lips. “You just suck, that’s all.”

“I suck like your mother be suckin’,” Marcus said.

Tyrel threw a closed fist over his mouth while Brian whispered, “Damn.”

“Whatever, Marcus. She’s your stank-ass mother too,” his sister shot back.

Another “damn” from Brian, while Tyrel turned and laughed.

“A’ight,” Will said, turning off the game. “Be out.”

Both siblings groaned, put their controllers down, and walked out of the room.

Before she walked through the door, Will’s little sister looked at Brian. “Hi, Brian,” she said, her voice singsong.

“Sup, Charmaine,” Brian said.

“You look nice,” Charmaine said.

“Charmaine, get your ass out of the fuckin’ room!” Will said sternly.

With that Charmaine hustled out.

Will slammed the door shut. “Fuckin’ fast ass, yo. I swear she gonna be pregnant by the time she hits fifteen.”

“Just keep her away from Brian and she might be a’ight,” Tyrel said, plopping down on the bed.

“Yeah, a’ight,” Brian said, sitting beside him.

Will grabbed a chair from a desk by the window and sat down. "Yo, Brian, stop acknowledging her ass when she talk to you. You be sendin' her in heat and shit."

"Yeah, OK," Brian replied.

The friends laughed for a few seconds, and then Tyrel cleared his throat. "A'ight, let's get this shit over with. I got shit to do tonight."

"Yeah, me too," Will said. "Shauntel's gonna meet me at Shawn's joint."

Brian and Tyrel looked at one another. Then Tyrel looked at Will and said, "You hit that shit yet, nigga?"

"Nah," Will said, the tone in his voice flat.

Tyrel laughed and gave Brian five. "Nigga, I told you, if you wanna lose your virginity, then you need to let that bitch's tight ass go."

Brian looked at his heavyset friend. "Yo, son, you a virgin for real?"

"Fuck no, I ain't a virgin," Will said, his beige-colored face turning a shade of red.

"Yeah, a'ight," Tyrel said.

Will clenched his jaw. "Man, I ain't no virgin," he insisted again.

Brian and Tyrel laughed while Will stewed in his chair. After a few more seconds of laughter at their friend's expense, they got down to the business at hand.

"A'ight, you niggas ready to do this shit?" Tyrel asked Brian and Will.

Will nodded. "More than ready, son."

Brian nodded, and took a deep breath and held it. No matter how many times they'd done this, he'd always gotten butterflies in the pit of his stomach. He was especially nervous this time, because of the .45s they each held, which he still didn't agree with, but Tyrel demanded they use. The knowledge that they weren't loaded was the only thing easing his mind. But still, if something went wrong and cops showed up and saw the guns . . . He quickly put his attention back on the matter at hand and shook that thought from his mind.

The three of them waited in the shadows across the street from the Laundromat. Waited and watched. After the last customer—a woman—struggled through the front door with a cart full of folded clothes, and headed down the block, the Laundromat's owner, a man Brian knew very well, Mr. Patel, moved to the front and pulled the shade down in front of the window.

Tyrel looked at his boys. "Showtime, niggas," he said, pulling his black ski mask down over his face. "We do this shit right, we'll be out in five minutes, a'ight?"

Will pulled his mask down, and said, "Cool."

Brian pulled his down also, but said nothing.

Tyrel took a quick glance up and down the block, then said, "Let's move!" and ran across the street, Will and Brian on his heels, and rushed into the cleaners before the owner could lock the doors.

"Get the fuck to the register and get the fuckin' money!" he ordered, pushing Mr. Patel backward.

Brian locked the door, and then stayed just off to the left, peeking through the side of the window shade, keeping watch for the police or any witnesses. *Five minutes,* he thought, his heart beating heavily.

Mr. Patel's wife, who had been checking the dryers for stray clothing, screamed out and tried to make a run for the back. But before she could make it, Will grabbed her by her long ponytail and pulled her to the ground. "Shut the fuck up and don't fuckin' move, bitch!" Frightened tears flooded immediately from her eyes as she whimpered and shivered.

Four minutes, Brian thought.

He took another peek to the outside. To their benefit, Jamaica Avenue was unusually quiet, which made him even more nervous. He looked at Tyrel, who had knocked the owner to the ground with his shoving. *Shit,* he thought.

He looked at the clock again. Three minutes, and they still didn't have the money.

Sweat trickled down the middle of his back, and his face began to itch beneath the mask. He nervously opened and closed his hands around the butt of the .45. He didn't like holding it at all.

Laughing hysterically, Will gyrated his hips, standing over Mrs. Patel as she continued to cry rivers, and then he made the ultimate mistake. "Yo, Brian, check this shit out, son."

Brian and Tyrel looked at one another in disbelief as time stood still.

Tyrel turned and glared hard at Will, who, realizing what he'd done, quickly looked down to the floor.

Tyrel shook his head and then pointed his unloaded weapon at Mr. Patel, who was pleading for his life in a language Tyrel didn't understand. He kicked the owner in the side. "Shut the fuck up, you fuckin' terrorist ma'fucka! And get the fuck up and get our money!"

Brian's body seemed to shake with each beat of his heart. His hands shook with adrenaline and nervousness.

His name.

Will had used his goddamned name. It wasn't an uncommon name, but still it was something to give to the police.

He took a quick peek to the outside. The coast was still clear, but they were losing time. *Five goddamned minutes,* he thought. He looked over at Will, who stood silently with slumped shoulders, pointing his weapon at Mrs. Patel's chest.

Mr. Patel scrambled up, and, with some help from a hard shove from Tyrel, went behind the counter. With trembling hands, he opened the register.

Before he could do anything else, Tyrel hit him across the forehead with his gun. He reached into the register and grabbed all of the money he could, and shoved it into a book bag he'd had over his shoulder.

"Let's get the fuck outta here!" he said, running past Brian and through the door.

They raced to the stairs leading up to the J train on Eldert's Lane. As they did, they removed their masks and stuffed those and the guns in their pants pockets.

"The train's here. Come on!" Tyrel yelled.

They raced up the steps, hopped the turnstiles, and made it onto the train just as the doors were beginning to close. As it pulled away, they all sat silent and winded.

Tyrel's eyes were fixed on Will, who kept his head down, while Brian leaned his head back and stared up at an advertisement for New York Metropolitan College.

They got off at the Broadway Junction exit, and, after walking as calmly as they could past police officers posted there, they headed to a side alley, where they dropped their masks in a Dumpster.

Tyrel took the guns from Will and Brian, dropped all three of them into the book bag with the money, and then before either of them could react, grabbed Will by his shirt collar and shoved him hard against the building's brick wall. "Nigga, what the fuck is your problem?"

His eyes wide, Will shook his head. His voice low and tight, he said, "My bad, son. The shit just slipped out."

"Just slipped out?" Tyrel said, shoving him back again. "Nigga . . ."

"Yo, come on, son," Will said, his eyes growing dark. "Let go of my collar."

Tyrel shook him and drove him back hard into the wall again. "Or what, nigga?"

Will looked at Tyrel, as Tyrel glared back at him.

"You wanna test me, nigga?" Tyrel seethed.

"I'm sayin', man," Will said. "Just let my shit go."

Brian shook his head. He could see the temper rising behind Will's eyes, while steam was already spilling from the top of Tyrel's head. In another second, things were going to go from bad to worse, and although Will had a nasty temper and could hold his own, he was no match for Tyrel.

He had to break it up.

"Yo, T, son, let him go," he said, stepping forward and placing his hand on Tyrel's shoulder.

His eyes still fixed on Will, Tyrel said, "This nigga said your name, son."

Brian looked at Will. "I know, man, but I ain't the only Brian around here. It was fuckin' stupid, but it's cool. It ain't worth getting into no shit over."

Will and Tyrel continued to stare one another down.

"Come on, son. Let him go. That's your boy."

Tyrel gritted his teeth, and then, after a few tense seconds, let go of Will's collar. "Yeah, a'ight." He looked at Brian. "We boys," he said. Then he turned back to Will. "Nigga, don't ever pull some shit like that again, you feel me?"

"I feel you," Will said regrettably. Then he looked at Brian. "Yo, my bad, son. It just slipped out, for real."

Brian nodded, then reached out and gave his boy a pound. "It's cool," he said.

"Make sure nothin' like that slips out again," Tyrel said.

"Yeah, a'ight," Will replied. "My bad, for real, son. I was trippin'. We cool?"

Tyrel looked at him for a short second, and then nodded. "We cool."

The two friends exchanged a one-armed hug.

"A'ight," Tyrel said when they parted. "Let's count this shit and be on our way."

After splitting $500, far less than what Tyrel had promised, they all went to Shawn's party, where Carla, who had found a way to get out of going to church with her mother, was waiting for Brian.

Frustrated over the stress they'd gone through for that little bit of money, Brian was glad to see her. He moved away from Will and Tyrel, and approached her. "Let's get out of here," he said, as Jay-Z blasted from the speakers.

Carla looked at him with raised eyebrows. "Hello to you too."

Brian smiled. "My bad." He pulled her close and gave her a kiss with a lot of tongue. "Hello," he said after a few seconds.

Carla smiled. "That's better. So what you wanna leave for? You just got here."

"I'm not in the mood," Brian answered.

"You don't wanna dance?" Carla asked.

"Nah," Brian said flatly. "I just wanna chill."

Carla looked into his eyes and could see that something was bothering him. She knew he got into things from time to time with Will and Tyrel, but she never asked for specifics. "OK," she said, taking his hand. "Let's go. My mother will be at church for at least another two hours."

Brian smiled and stirred in his jeans. "Sounds like a plan," he said.

5

Deahnna opened her eyes, stretched, and then took a glance over at her alarm clock. As was always the case, she was ahead of the alarm by fifteen minutes. She stretched again, feeling her calves and shoulders pop, and then reached across her night table and flipped off the switch on her clock. Her body's internal clock always woke her every morning at 6:00 A.M., no matter what time she went to bed. Setting the alarm clock—a clock she'd paid too damned much for—hadn't been necessary, but on the off chance that her body demanded more sleep, she continued to do it.

She took a final stretch, and then swung her legs off of the bed. It was Saturday. Her cleaning day. Her two-bedroom apartment was never really messy, but because she spent the majority of her weekly hours going between two jobs, she had just enough time—and, more importantly, energy—to tidy during the week. Just as they had been for her mother, Deahnna always devoted Saturday mornings to cleaning from top to bottom. Sweeping, dusting, wiping, vacuuming, washing, scrubbing, scraping; dust, mold, grease, and grime were all dealt with in a major way.

Deahnna yawned, and then rose from her queen-sized bed, grabbed her silk kimono from the hook on her closet door, and made her way to the bathroom to brush her teeth and wash her face. She applied toothpaste to her Sonic toothbrush, turned on the water, and paused as she caught a glimpse of a pair of slightly slanted dark brown eyes staring back at her from the mirror.

Deahnna sighed.

The average person would stare into the mirror and see exactly what she was—a very young-looking thirty-two-year-old. The average person wouldn't see the wrinkles creeping away from the corners of her eyes, the ever so faint stress lines running across her forehead. The average person wouldn't see the sadness, the pain she'd endured. The average person wouldn't see the years of struggling, of doing what she had to do to get by for herself and her son. The average person wouldn't see the disappointment.

Life was supposed to be different, she thought. *So very different.* But circumstances and challenges had arisen to chase dreams away. Deahnna wouldn't change the outcome of those circumstances if given the chance, but she damn sure would have delayed them for about six or seven years.

She expelled a breath again.

Things, and the decisions she'd had to make, weren't ideal, but they were necessary to make life what it was, which, compared to a lot of other people she knew, was golden. But despite the way things were, Deahnna was determined to see them change. She just had to grin and bear the hurdles in her path. It wasn't easy, and some days were better than others, but slowly, and surely, she would see things change.

They just had to.

She sighed again, and then turned on her toothbrush and got rid of the plaque and morning breath. She washed her face, and then after inspecting and clearing a small pimple on her cheek, she went to the kitchen and put on some hot water to boil for a morning cup of tea. As the water boiled, she went back to her bedroom. On her way, she paused outside of her son's closed bedroom door.

She was tempted to open it and wake him up to make him clean the filth she knew was inside, but she decided to cut him some slack and give him another hour of sleep. She was sure he needed it, as he'd undoubtedly been up 'til God knew what time, playing his Xbox.

She smiled as she thought about her son. A positive to come from a very negative situation, his existence had been unplanned, but never unwanted. Well, not by her, anyway. She loved her son. Had from the first moment she laid eyes on him. He was her best friend, her confidant, her protector, just as she was his.

Within the past couple of years, things had become strained between them, but Deahnna knew that had to do with his yearning to fly away from the nest, and her desire to keep him there safe. In time, she supposed, that would pass. Or hoped it would.

She put her palm lightly on his door and thought about the times when he refused to sleep in his own bed. Things were harder back then, but he hadn't known it. He also hadn't known that he provided the only source of light in her world for her to see. She wanted to push his door open and rush to his bed, dig him out from beneath his New York Giants comforter, wrap her arms around him, and wet his cheek with kisses. But, of course, she knew her outpouring of love would be met with a "Come on, Mom!" and a quick nosedive for safety, back beneath the comforter.

That made her smile. And it also made her wrap her hand around the doorknob. She began to turn it. And then paused as the front door opened.

She turned her head to see the son she had just known was sleeping soundly in his room walk into the apartment.

"What the hell?" She let go of the doorknob. "Brian, what are you doing walking in here right now?"

Brian sighed, and as the door closed behind him, he said, "Mom—"

But his mother cut him off. "I don't see any bags in your hand, but you better tell me that you just came from the store."

"Mom—"

"You know what time I expect you home, Brian."

"I know, Mom, I just—"

"Then why are you just now walking through that door at six A.M.?"

Brian groaned and walked slowly to his room.

Deahnna gave her son a hard glare as he walked past her. It was a stare that used to bring tears to his eyes, but now did little more than make him frown. She folded her arms across her chest as he opened his door and walked into his room, which, to her surprise, was actually clean. "So, I'm waiting for my explanation."

"If you'd let me speak, Mom, I would answer you."

Deahnna slit her eyes and pointed a slender index finger at her son. "Boy, don't get fresh with me, you understand?"

Brian groaned again, and then said, "Sorry."

Deahnna pressed her lips together firmly. "Mm-hmm. So where were you?"

"I . . . I was over at Tyrel's crib."

"Boy, you can speak your slang all you want in the streets, but in this house, it's only proper English I want to hear."

Brian let out another groan. "I was at Tyrel's house playing Xbox with him and Will. I ended up falling asleep."

"Brian, you know how I feel about you being with Will and Tyrel. Especially Tyrel."

"Mom—"

"I hear things about them, you know. I hear about the trouble they like to get into. Especially Tyrel."

"People talk bullsh . . ." Brian paused, catching himself quickly. "People don't know what they're talking about. Trust me, more than half the time the trouble Tyrel gets into is him just defending himself."

"Mm-hmm."

"For real, Mom. Why do you trip out so much about them? You know them."

"Exactly. I do know them."

"They're my boys."

"I understand that, Brian. I just don't understand why you've never found other boys to hang out with. Boys who have real futures ahead of them like you do, unlike Tyrel."

Brian slammed his fist down on his bed. "Why do you always judge Tyrel like that? You don't even take the time to talk to him. You have no clue what he's about. What he's into."

"You're wrong, Brian. I do know what Tyrel is into. It's the same thing he was into when he was a little boy: trouble. Tyrel has been and will always be a roughneck with a nigger mentality. And I promise you, Brian, if you don't stop hanging around him, he's going to get you into something that you won't be able to get out of."

"Damn, Mom. I'm seventeen years old!"

"And?"

"I'm practically a man. I can handle myself."

Deahnna couldn't help but laugh. "Trust me, dear, you're getting older, but you're far from being a man."

"Yeah, well, I'm more man than the nigga you got wit' to produce me."

Without thought or hesitation, Deahanna stepped toward her son and slapped him hard across his face. "What did I tell you about using that language around me? I'm not one of your boys, Brian. I am your mother and you *will* respect me as that. And for your information, I didn't just *get wit'* your father. I was young, yes, but I was in love. I'm not proud of the man I chose, but that mistake gave me you, and I am proud that you were the end result of my bad choice."

Brian stood silent with his eyes slit and his lips tight.

Deahanna hated to see that face; he looked too much like his father.

She shook her head and frowned. She wanted to say more, but knew it would just be a waste of her breath. "Clean this room," she said, despite how neat it was. "And when you're done, go and do the bathroom, and then vacuum."

Without another word, she walked off into her bedroom and slammed the door shut behind her.

She sat down heavily on her bed. She hadn't meant to hit him, but his statement about getting with his father had stung. She'd only been sixteen, but she'd loved his father, Terrance, with all her heart. He was her first love, her first real boyfriend. He was twenty-one and rough around the edges, but with Deahnna he'd always been gentle, kind. And when he would look in her eyes and tell her that she was his everything, she believed it. Never in a million years did she ever think that he would hurt her, but he had. Twice.

The first time was when he raped her.

They were at her apartment alone; her mother was working a double shift. They were in her bedroom, sitting on her bed, kissing and fondling each other as they always did. She was a virgin and Terrance had always seemed to be OK with that. Whenever he tried to take the fondling and kissing further, all Deahnna ever had to say was no, and he would back off, saying that he could and would wait because he loved her. But that day he'd apparently had enough. He wanted to be inside of her. Deahnna tried to push him off of her as he started to become forceful, but he'd been too strong. That day he wasn't taking no for an answer. He was dead set on taking what he wanted. After it happened,

Deahnna blamed herself for the incident. Telling herself that she'd let the touching and kissing go too far, and because of that, she'd taken Terrance to the point of no return.

She never told anyone about what had happened, and, weeks later, she discovered that she was pregnant. She hadn't seen or heard from Terrance since that day. Calls and knocks on his door went unanswered. His boys didn't seem to know where he was. Eventually, she did manage to track him down. This would be the second time he hurt her.

When she told him the news about the baby, he denied it was his. He accused her of having sex with somebody else, which, of course, had been a lie, since her virgin blood had been all left behind on the sheets of her bed. He cursed her out, called her all kinds of derogatory names, and then told her to stay the fuck away from him. Heartbroken, Deahnna was forced to deal with having to break the news to her mother on her own. Her mother, having been through something similar in her past, wanted her to have an abortion, but Deahnna didn't believe in them. Because she'd refused, her mother kicked her out of the house. She lived at a friend's house for a few weeks, and then eventually moved in with her mother's estranged sister, who helped her finish high school. Deahanna moved out when she was nineteen, and it had been she and Brian ever since.

Because Brian looked just like him, Terrance remained a constant on Deahnna's mind. One day, through the grapevine in the neighborhood, she found out that she hadn't been the only woman he'd raped. A fifteen-year-old girl was brave enough to come forward, and told a similar story. Another sixteen-year-old came after that. Terrance was now in jail in Rikers Island, and Deahnna hoped he was getting done to him what had been done to her and the other females.

"Practically a man." She shook her head. In another year, in the eyes of the law, Brian would be just that. A man who'd have to deal with the good and bad consequences of life. She wanted to shelter him forever from bad, but knew that she couldn't, and that was maddeningly frustrating.

She closed her eyes and squeezed her temples. "Why couldn't he have just been in the damn room?"

6

A high school dance.

It had been a long time since he'd attended one. Since his own high school days, actually.

Jawan looked around the gym, which was packed—something that surprised him. When he was in high school, there hadn't been much for him and his friends to do besides roam around King's Plaza, hang out at a friend's house, or just run the streets. They didn't have all of the under-twenty-one hangout spots like they had now, so when they were on, the dances were the place to be. Dances were where you came with your boyfriend or girlfriend to get the tight squeeze when the slow jams were played—something the current DJs no longer did.

As the kids these days were all too grown and too cool, Jawan found the turnout to be really surprising. He surmised that kids must have either really missed the gatherings, as the school had cancelled them for a few years due to excessive violence in the past, or they just had as little to do as he had when he was their age.

Jawan looked around at the kids dancing in the middle of the gymnasium's floor, as the kids twitched as though their bodies were on fire and infested with fleas, snapped and leaned as if they had rhythmic Tourette's syndrome, or just did things that belonged in bedrooms behind closed doors. Their dances made no sense to him, and some just looked painful and clumsy. They weren't graceful or smooth like the cabbage patch, the run-joe, the running man, or the Kid 'n Play.

Now those were moves.

And so were the ones done when break dancing. Something to Jawan's surprise and pleasure that many of the guys in the middle of the floor were doing now. He smiled as some of the quietest students he'd seen roaming the halls, pop-locked and windmilled while their peers cheered them on.

For a moment, he was tempted to venture out and show off the moves he used to do on flattened cardboard and wide pieces of linoleum. They'd be blown away by his skills, he knew. They'd probably come clamoring to him for lessons, but his schedule just wouldn't allow it. Nor would his body, which he knew would fight him tooth and nail to keep from doing things and getting into positions it knew it had no business even attempting.

For a fleeting moment, he wished, for one night, he could invert the numbers of his age. But as it was, he was thirty-two, and although the decline down the hill was slow going, it was downhill regardless.

So much for getting old, he kidded to himself.

He walked around the gym slowly. The DJ was actually playing some half-decent tracks that had his head moving to the beat. The music wasn't as moving as what he'd grown up with, but it was cool.

He tapped and observed the students who weren't on the dance floor. Some congregated in small, tight circles against the walls. Others were couples holding hands. Like Brian and Carla.

Jawan paused when he saw his student. He smiled. It was nice to see that he'd come and hadn't gotten into any li'l somethin's for the night. In some ways, Brian reminded Jawan of himself. Smart, good-looking, quiet on the outside, yet troubled on the inside. Brian had a lot of potential, and although he'd never spoken about his dreams or goals, Jawan knew he had them.

Jawan hadn't grown up with a male presence at home,

but he'd grown up in a time when li'l somethin's were things that the majority of the time could be walked away from. Times were different now, and unfortunately far too many kids were getting caught up in li'l somethin's that they weren't walking away from ever again.

Jawan knew that his role and influence were limited, but he was determined to have some sort of an effect on Brian.

He watched as Brian led Carla to the dance floor as Jamie Foxx's instant classic, "Blame It," began to play. Off to his right, someone said, "They didn't play songs like that at my school dances."

Jawan turned his head.

A woman stood a few inches away from him, her arms folded tightly across her chest. Her lips were pressed firmly together as she shook her head. He'd only met her once, but he'd never forgotten her soft eyes, capturing smile, or her curvaceous, toned figure.

Brian's mother.

He'd first laid eyes on her two years ago in the office of the school, when she came to meet with the principal after Brian had gotten into trouble for fighting. Jawan had been getting papers from his mail slot. He didn't know who she was, but she had captivated him instantly, and he had actually hoped to have Brian for a student one day just so that he'd have a chance to meet her. But, of course, the meeting wouldn't have really mattered because she would have been his student's mother, and, because of that, it would have been brief and very professional.

And now here she was, standing beside him, inches away, looking stunning, dressed simply in a beige sweater and a pair of dark blue jeans with black boots on her feet, and her hair lying around her shoulders.

Jawan took a breath and said, "It's a good song."

Deahnna Moore turned toward him. “He’s singing about alcohol making him feel loose,” she said.

Jawan laughed. “It’s a harmless song.”

“Mm-hmm. You say that now. But just wait until your daughter or son is singing about blaming their actions on alcohol.”

Jawan laughed again, as did Deahnna. After a few seconds, he stuck out his hand. “Jawan White.”

Deahnna took it, smiled, and said, “Deahnna Moore.”

Jawan nodded in Brian’s direction. “I’m Brian’s English teacher.”

“Nice to meet you,” she said, smiling again. “I hope Brian doesn’t give you a hard time in class. He’s going through a phase right now. The kind where he thinks he knows it all.”

Jawan shook his head. “He’s no trouble at all. He’s got a good head on his shoulders. You’ve done a great job with him.”

Deahnna smiled. “Thank you. It’s just me at home. I do the best I can.”

“I wish you could do the best you could for a lot of my other students,” Jawan said sincerely.

“Thank you,” Deahnna said again.

“My pleasure.”

“So, Mr. White—”

“Jawan, please.”

“OK. Jawan. So are you chaperoning?”

Jawan nodded. “I am. My arm kind of got twisted into it by my boss. Kind of had no choice.”

“I’d say so.”

“But I’m actually having a good time. I didn’t expect to see so many of the kids here. What about yourself? I assume you’re chaperoning also.”

Deahnna gave a nod. “I overheard him on the phone talking about this dance to his girlfriend, and how big of a deal it was since Lane hadn’t had one in a while.

I figured coming here would be a way to see who his girlfriend was, so I called the school and volunteered."

Jawan looked toward the floor. The DJ was playing a Ne-Yo track now, and while everyone was still dancing, their bodies were just a little closer. "You don't have to worry. Her name's Carla and she's a good girl. Just like Brian, she focuses on her schoolwork and gets good grades."

"That's good to know." Deahnna sighed. "I wish all of his friends were that way."

"Believe me," Jawan said, his eyes back on her, "I talk to him all the time about the company he keeps."

"Well, I'm glad someone else does besides me. I know I sound like a broken record when I speak to him about his"—she put up her fingers and made air quotation marks—"boys."

"I'm sure I sound just as broken," Jawan said, "But you have to keep talking, you know."

"I definitely know."

"Brian's a smart kid. He just needs a reminder sometimes to help keep his head on straight. All kids do. I don't know about you, but I know I did."

"So you were a troublemaker, huh?" Deahnna said with a smile.

Jawan shook his head. "Not really a troublemaker. I just went through a period trying to find myself. You know, the old hanging with the wrong crowd trying to be part of the in-crowd thing. Did some things I'm not proud of."

"And look at you now," Deahnna said, staring at him with a smile.

"Luckily I had an uncle who stepped into my life at the right time to rein me in when I'd become too much for my mother to handle."

Deahnna nodded. "The power of a male presence," she said with a touch of sadness in her voice.

Jawan looked at her. "I take it Brian's father isn't around?"

Deahnna raised her eyebrows and frowned. "Never was," she said bluntly.

Jawan looked back to Brian, who was laughing playfully as he twirled Carla around. "Wherever he is, he's missing out on a special kid," he said genuinely.

"He's locked up," Deahnna said bluntly. "He's missing out on a hell of a lot. And he will for a very long time."

Jawan turned and looked at her closely. She didn't need to give any more information than she had for him to see that she'd been hurt somehow by Brian's father. He could hear it beneath the strength in her voice. There was hurt there. He turned and looked back to Brian. *Maybe a seventeen-year hurt,* he surmised.

He turned and gave Deahnna a smile. She was truly captivating. Although he didn't know her well, he felt a desire to reach out and hold her close. A need to protect her.

Deahnna watched him as he studied her. And then her eyes grew wide. "I love this song!" she exclaimed.

The DJ had just started playing "Single Ladies" by Beyoncé. It was a hit from the previous year, but just like Jamie Foxx's song, it was a classic.

Jawan laughed. "That's the ladies' anthem."

Deahnna began to move her hips and shoulders to the groove. Jawan watched her, and felt a stirring in his jeans. Her moves were subtle, but almost sensual. "I'm a big Beyoncé fan," she said.

Jawan nodded. "Yeah. I'm a fan too," he said with a sneaky glint in his eye.

Deahnna looked at him. "Mm-hmm. I bet you are."

Jawan shrugged one shoulder. "Hey, Beyoncé's got, um . . . skills."

Deahnna gave him another "Mm-hmm."

Jawan laughed and watched as she lost herself in the

song and did a turn. As she did, someone came behind him and whispered, “Watch those eyes, Mr. White.”

Jawan turned around to see Brian walking off backward, giving him the “I’m watching you” motion that Robert DeNiro made famous in the movie *Meet the Parents*. Jawan gave him a nod and did his own “I’m watching you” motion, and then turned back to Deahnna.

She was fanning herself. “I get caught up when I hear that song.”

“Believe me,” Jawan said, adding a touch of machismo to his voice, “it was all good. You really don’t have to stop on my account.”

Deahnna looked at him with a slight rise in the corner of her mouth. “Is that right?”

Jawan nodded. “Most definitely.”

Deahnna looked at him for a lingering second, and then gave another “Mm-hmm.”

Jawan laughed. “So, Deahnna, would you like something to drink?”

“Do they serve mojitos here?”

Jawan chuckled. “I don’t know what I can do about the mojitos, but I know I can get you a slamming bottle of water.”

Deahnna laughed. “Water will be fine,” she said.

“Be right back.”

Jawan walked away, and as he did, he couldn’t help but smile. There was definitely a very strong and very mutual attraction going on. He had his policy about students’ mothers, but still, he couldn’t keep his mind from wondering what it would be like to see her again, outside of school.

He got the water with that thought on his mind. When he came back, Deahnna was watching her son on the floor. “Trust me,” Jawan said, handing her a bottle, “your son has good taste.”

Deahnna thanked him for the water. "I work so much. I'm looking at him now just thinking about how much of his life I'm missing out on. Yesterday we had a disagreement and he said to me that he was practically a man. I told him he was far from being a man, but looking at him now . . ." She paused and gave a half shake with her head. "He's growing so damned fast. I want so much for him."

"So do I," Jawan said. "He's a really great kid. I think he's going to be just fine," he said reassuringly.

Deahnna smiled, took a sip of her water, and continued to watch her son.

A few minutes of silence passed between them. As they did, Jawan watched her with keen eyes. *Off-limits,* he told himself. It didn't matter how sexy she was. It didn't matter how intriguing, or how much she stirred his senses. Senses that had been dulled since Kim.

She's Brian's mother.

He's your student.

She's off-limits.

Off.

Limits.

Move on.

He watched her, and, suddenly, as if reading his mind, she turned and looked at him and smiled.

Dammit.

She was wrong for that.

Before he could stop himself, he said, "Maybe someday I can treat you to that mojito."

Deahnna closed her eyes a bit and then smiled. "Someday might be nice," she said.

Jawan gave her a nod, then took a sip of his own bottle and turned back to look at his students. *Policy? What policy?* he thought.

They were both chaperoning the dance, yet for the rest of the night, neither he nor Deahnna moved from where they stood. They chatted some more about light topics, and then, before they parted ways, they exchanged phone numbers.

"Policy be damned," Jawan said later that night to Grady, who lay with him on his bed, watching ESPN.

In his dreams later on, with the crashing waves, and the moonlight, it wasn't Janet Jackson he was caressing. It was Deahnna Moore. And in the background, Beyoncé's song was playing.

7

Brian sat quietly in his seat, waiting for the bell to ring. Unlike any other day, he had no plans to rush out of the classroom. He wanted to have a conversation with his English teacher. There was something that he needed to make clear. He'd seen the way Mr. White had been talking with his mom. More importantly, he'd seen the way he'd looked at her.

So had his friends.

And they hadn't hesitated to comment about it at the dance, after the dance, via text message the next day, and all day during school. All of the chattering and sarcastic comments had been getting on his fucking nerves. So he waited for the bell to help his teacher understand . . .

His mom was off-limits to everyone.

There was nothing personal against Mr. White. It was just a rule that he'd set in stone when he was six years old. That was when he'd first begun to ask questions about his father's existence. Who was he? Was he still alive? If he was, why wasn't he around? Didn't he love them? Was he mad at them?

They were innocent questions. Questions that, at six years old, Brian expected to be answered. But they never were. Eventually Brian stopped asking, and the older he got, the more it became evident to him that his mother's unwillingness to provide even the simplest of answers had been because, at some point in time, the man who'd given his sperm to create him had hurt her badly.

Because of that, Brian refused to let any man get close to her, and so as the years passed, he did whatever he had to do to sabotage any relationships she tried to have, by letting the men know with either words or actions that their presence was unwanted. How well they treated his mother never mattered, because in his eyes, they had the potential to bring his mother more pain.

Mr. White was cool, and seemed to be a good and, to a certain extent, trustworthy man. Brian had actually allowed the wall that masked the pain he'd felt from being a bastard child to come down a notch, because he appreciated the fact that, other than his mother, his teacher had been the only other person in his life who was constantly on his ass about him doing the right thing for his future. Brian put up resistance to the talks because, well, he couldn't just make things that easy, and he also wanted to do things his way. But he appreciated the talks nonetheless.

Deep down he believed that Mr. White had nothing but good intentions, but Brian still owed it to his mother to let the man know what was up. Whatever thoughts Mr. White had in his head concerning his mother, he needed to let them go quickly.

When the bell rang he would send that message loud and clear.

His cell phone buzzed in his pocket suddenly. Brian looked to make sure Mr. White hadn't noticed, as cell phones were prohibited, and when he was sure that he hadn't, he pulled his phone out to see a text message from Tyrel:

Meet me an' Will at pizza shop. Wanna talk more bidness.

Brian looked up at the clock on the wall above the classroom door. School would be over in five minutes.

Discreetly, he replied:

A'ight. But I'ma B a minute. Gotta do somethin'.

Seconds later, Tyrel responded:

A'ight then meet me at Will's crib at 7.

Brian replied that he would, and then slipped the phone back into his pocket. As he did, he wondered about what business Tyrel wanted to discuss. After the way things had gone down with the Laundromat, he was surprised Tyrel even wanted to be around Will. They'd had little beefs here and there growing up, but things had never been as bad as they'd been that night. There'd been a look in Tyrel's eyes that made Brian feel that had the .45s been loaded, something very tragic would have happened. Will had challenged him in a way he never had before, and that surprised Brian.

Business.

The business that night hadn't really been for shit, and that frustrated Brian. But Carla had helped to ease that frustration. So much so that he couldn't bring himself to leave her side before her mother came home, so he hid in her closet until her mother went to bed, and then spent the rest of the night holding her in his arms. He'd slept longer than he intended, and he had to hightail the two blocks home, trying to beat his mother's early rise.

Of course, he hadn't.

At the party after the Laundromat heist, Tyrel and Will were cool, but the tension had been thick between them and they'd barely spoken to one another. Brian hoped that when he got to Will's later that night, things would be back to normal.

The bell rang for dismissal. Brian waited for the other students to hustle out, and then approached his teacher, who was erasing the chalkboard. "Mr. White, you got a second?"

His teacher turned around and looked down at his watch. "Sure," he said. "I have about fifteen minutes to spare."

"Cool. This won't take too long. I just wanna talk about somethin' really quick."

Mr. White nodded, and then sat down on the edge of his desk. "What's up?"

Brian cleared his throat. "I just wanted to talk about the dance on Saturday."

His teacher smiled. "It was fun," he said. "It looked like you and Carla had a good time."

Brian gritted his teeth as his teacher continued to smile. He couldn't help but think he was smiling because of his mother. "Yeah," he said unenthusiastically. "It was cool."

"So, what's going on?"

Brian gave his teacher a hard stare. "Remember when I said I was watching you?"

Mr. White nodded and laughed. "I remember."

Brian wasn't smiling as he said, "Mr. White, you're a cool dude, and I have mad respect for you, but I'ma need for you to leave my mom alone."

His teacher's smile dropped instantly. "Excuse me?"

Brian straightened his back as he puffed out his chest a little. "Look, it's nothing personal, but I have to look out for my mom. She has enough to deal with, and the last thing she needs right now is for some nigga to be pressing up on her."

Mr. White raised a single eyebrow and folded his arms across his chest. He looked at Brian for a cool couple of seconds before speaking. "Look, Brian, first things first, I'm no nigga. So save that for your boys. Second, as out of line as it is, I respect what you're trying to do. You're looking out for your mother's best interests and that's honorable."

"My mom—" Brian started.

"Your mother is a grown woman, Brian. And she's free to talk to whomever she chooses. She knows more than you do what she has on her plate. Now, as I said,

I respect your intentions. You care about your mother and don't want anyone hurting her. I get it. And if I were in your position, I might do the same thing, although a little differently. But let me assure you, I'm not out to hurt your mother. As a matter of fact, I'm not out for anything at all. We talked, we enjoyed each other's company, and we said good-bye. End of story. Now, do yourself a favor and don't approach me this way again. I'm your teacher, and, more importantly, I'm a man who demands respect, and believe me, the last thing I'm going to do is sit here and listen to you warn me about who I'm allowed to interact with."

"You—"

"We're done, Mr. Moore. I have somewhere I need to be, and you need to be somewhere else."

Brian flared his nostrils and stared at his teacher. Aside from his mother, no one had ever gotten away with speaking to him in that manner. He'd never allowed it. He wanted to be mad. Hell, he should have been. But as he watched his teacher, who was watching him with just as intense a glare, Brian felt something that surprised him.

Admiration.

Mr. White had kept it very real with him, and Brian couldn't help but have respect for that.

He took a breath and let it out slowly. "A'ight," he said with a nod.

Mr. White nodded back, said, "Good," and then held out a closed fist for a pound.

Brian looked at his fist and then at him.

"Are you going to leave me hanging or what?" his teacher asked.

Brian looked at him for a second longer and then shook his head. *I definitely have to respect him,* he thought. He said, "Nah," and then dapped his teacher.

"Listen, Brian, you having your mother's back is a

good thing, OK? But I want you to think about something: your mother's happiness. It's obvious she was dealt a bad hand with your father—you both were—but he was only one bad apple. I know it's not easy, but you're going to have to learn to step back and let your mother live. She needs that, and, quite frankly, she deserves it, too. Now you're her son, her first man, and no one will ever be closer to her than you are. But the company you provide for her can only go so far. Believe it or not, there are good men out there, and you need to back off and give your mother opportunities to find one, or else she just might miss out on something. More importantly, you might too. OK?"

Brian nodded. "OK."

"Cool. I'll see you on Wednesday."

"A'ight." Brian turned to leave, but before he exited the classroom, Mr. White called out to him.

"Hey, Brian, hold on a sec."

Brian turned around. "Yeah?"

"Did you hear about what happened at Patel's Laundromat this past Friday night?"

Brian's heartbeat took a pause as he looked back at Mr. White, who was watching him closely. He said, "Yeah. I heard."

Mr. White shook his head and frowned. "Mr. Patel claims that three young black men with ski masks robbed him. He also said that one of the three yelled out the name Brian."

"Oh, word?"

"Yeah. The police came in this morning to get a listing on all of the Brians in the school. I think they're going to try to seek them out and ask questions."

"Lot of Brians here at Lane," Brian said.

His teacher nodded and kept his eyes on him. "Just figured I'd tell you so you're not surprised if you're approached."

"Good lookin'," Brian said.

His teacher stared at him. Brian looked away, the glare making him uncomfortable.

"You're making sure to avoid getting into any li'l somethin's with your boys, right?"

Brian nodded. "Yeah."

"I see you on Jamaica with them sometimes. Tyrel and another kid. What's his name?"

"Will," Brian answered reluctantly.

"Will Banks. That's right. He's older than you and Tyrel, right? He used to be a student here but he dropped out."

"Yeah," Brian said. "He's got his brother and sister to support."

"Must be hard on him financially."

"He's holding things down."

His teacher looked at him.

Brian looked away again, and cracked a couple of knuckles on his hand.

Walking back behind his desk, Mr. White said, "Stay out of trouble, Brian."

Brian nodded and, without a word, quickly walked out of the room. When he got outside, he wiped nervous sweat from his forehead. The police had his name. "Will, you fuckin' damn-ass nigga."

He shook his head.

At seven he would meet with Will and Tyrel to discuss business. They wouldn't like it, but the three-man cartel was going to lose a member.

8

"So, how was the school dance? Did you meet any sexy eligible bachelors? And I don't mean students."

Deahnna laughed and looked at her friend of twenty years in the mirror in front of her. Had she met any eligible bachelors? She smiled as her mind went back to the Friday night dance and Jawan White. Brian's teacher. She still couldn't believe she'd flirted with him the way she had. That had been completely out of character for her. Being open with a man just wasn't something Deahnna ever was. Brian's father, and then an ex after him, showed her that being open only meant being open to heartache, to pain. Love, she realized as years passed, was highly overrated. And because it was, she kept her heart sealed airtight, and her emotions in check. She'd been a fool twice, and she'd be damned if she'd be taken for one again.

But Friday night.

She hadn't been open, but, damn, the door had certainly creaked ajar ever so slightly, and, for the life of her, Deahnna couldn't figure out why. It wasn't as though she hadn't met attractive men before, because she certainly had, so she couldn't say that Jawan's looks had been the sole reason. And it wasn't as though she'd never met anyone else who was charming, either.

So why?

If not for his non-threatening, but very good, looks, his disarmingly sexy smile, his ass, which she'd taken a moment to check out as he went to get her some water, or his personable and genuine lighthearted personality, then what had it been about him that had given her the chills? What about him had put her so at ease and made her feel almost safe around him? The topic of significant others had never come up, but he hadn't been wearing a ring on his finger, which Deahnna knew meant nothing. So what about Mr. Jawan White had prompted her to take his phone number?

Had she met any eligible bachelors?

Deahnna looked at her friend, Heather, lifted a shoulder, raised her eyebrows, and said, "I don't know."

Heather Rose looked at her quizzically. "What do you mean you don't know?" She planted her hands on her wide hips, one hand gripping a styling comb, and said, "You either did or didn't."

For Heather, life was all about the yeas or nays, dos or don'ts. "To be's" or "not to be's." There were no uncertainties with her. If she was going to do something, she did it. If she was going to say something, she just said it. And if she was feeling something for someone, she didn't take the time to analyze and try to figure out if what she was feeling was real or not, she just felt it and went for it. In Heather's mind, the world was black and white. There were no shades of gray with her.

Although Heather's "it was or it wasn't" mentality had brought her a few bumps and bruises along the way to happiness, Deahnna often wished she could have been more like her at times. But life experiences had made Deahnna a thinker, a contemplator.

"So?" Heather pressed, spinning Deahnna around in the styling chair she was planted in.

Deahnna hesitated for a pensive moment, and then smiled. "I did."

Heather smiled, exposing a gap between her two front teeth. "Aw, shit!" she said. "I want details, honey. Now!"

"Yes," someone said from a chair to Heather's right. "Details!"

Heather rolled her eyes, sucked her teeth, and looked over. "Excuse you, Rico, but I don't remember ever hearing anyone say, 'Rico, please be a part of this conversation.'"

Rico Rose, whose real name was Richard, but who insisted on being called Rico, gave Heather a scowl. "Uh, excuse you, sister dear, but we all know that, I, Rico Suave, need no invitation. Nothing is sacred to these ears."

Heather rolled her eyes again. "Yes, we all know, queen Dumbo. It's hard for anything to be kept sacred from those big-ass flappers. Now, kindly A, B, C your way out of our conversation."

Deahnna and the other two clients inside of Heather's styling salon laughed out loud.

Rico rolled his eyes at his sister, and then looked at Deahnna. "Excuse me, Deahnna, while *someone* over there chooses to be a rude ass, can you please enlighten us as to whom it is who has you open?"

"I didn't say he has me open," Deahnna said.

"Yes, brother dear, she didn't say all that."

Rico "hmph'd." "Sister dear, please. Deahnna is interested in a man. Shit, she may as well be open, because you know that don't happen."

Heather nodded. "OK," she said. "I will give you that." She looked back to Deahnna. "So speak, girl. Who has you open?"

Deahanna shook her head. "As I said, I'm not open. I'm just . . . intrigued."

"What's his name?" Heather asked.

"Jawan White."

Heather thought about it for a moment. "Nope. Never heard of him before."

"Neither have I," Rico said.

Deahnna looked at him. “Trust me, Rico, he doesn’t hang out on your side of the playground.”

Rico raised his eyebrows. “You’d be surprised to find out who does,” he said. “I could give you some stories.”

“The only thing we want you to give, brother dear,” Heather cut in, “is your attention back to Marie’s hair.”

Rico rolled his eyes again as his client, Marie, nodded and said, “Amen.”

“So, girl, tell me about this Jawan White.”

Deahnna smiled. “He teaches eleventh grade English.”

“Is he cute?”

Deahnna nodded. “Very. And he’s very nice, too. Seems really genuine and down to earth.”

“Hmm. Is he taken?”

Deahnna shook her head. “I don’t think so. I didn’t see a ring on his finger.”

“Means nothing,” Rico cut in as he braided Marie’s hair. “I know plenty of men with rings on their fingers.”

“I would tell him to butt out, but he’s right,” Heather said.

“I know,” Deahnna agreed. “But, as I said, one, he doesn’t play for that team, and two, I really think he’s unattached.”

“Hmm,” Heather said. “Good-looking, nice, easy to talk to, possibly single, and he’s intelligent. So . . . what’s wrong with him?”

“What do you mean what’s wrong with him?” Deahnna asked.

Heather sucked her teeth. “Girl, you know you’ll find something wrong with him sooner or later. You always do.”

“I just have high standards.”

“Girl, you don’t have high standards. You have ridiculous standards.”

“Not ridiculous, Heather. I just don’t want to settle. I don’t need any more Terrances or Marcs in my life. Especially the Terrances.”

"I know what you went through with Terrance was hard, and I know Marc really hurt you, but it's in the past now. It's time for you to stop blocking happiness, girl. There are more good men than there are Terrances or Marcs in this world."

Deahnna frowned. Terrance had raped her physically and mentally, and the emotional scars had taken a lot longer than the physical scars to heal. But Brian helped to absorb all of the pain and hurt, and eventually she found a way to move on. And when she did, Marc came into her life. Just like Jawan, he was an attractive man, with a sexy smile and a nice personality, though a little possessive. But Deahnna hadn't minded much, because after going so long without love, it just felt good to be with someone who was attentive. But nine months into the relationship, she discovered that Marc was married with three kids. Deahnna gave up on love after that.

"Listen, being cautious is a good thing, D. But as unfair as life can be sometimes, you only get one chance at it. So if there's really nothing wrong with the brother, I say you should just go for it."

"I second that," Rico said.

Deahnna said, "I know you're right."

"OK, then," Heather said.

"But there might be one thing wrong with him."

"Oh, Lord. We knew you'd find something," Heather said.

"Well . . . It's not a major, major issue, but it is something."

"So what is it?"

"He's one of Brian's teachers."

"I see. How does Brian feel about him?"

"I don't know. He's never mentioned him or any of his teachers to me. Of course, we don't really talk anymore like we used to."

"Don't worry. That will change after his teenage years."

"I hope so."

"He's just feeling himself. Thinks he's a man now, I'm sure."

"Oh, definitely," Deahnna said, thinking about her argument with him.

"Terri went through that with her son. Things were bad for a while, but once Freddie got out of high school, things started to get better. Same thing went for Erica and her son."

"Well I can't wait to get past this phase," Deahnna said. "Hopefully I'll still have my hair."

"Don't worry about that, girl," Heather said. "I can always hook you up with some good yak hair."

"Ew. No, thank you!"

Both women laughed, as did Rico and Maria. The third client was sitting beneath a dryer and hadn't heard anything.

"Anyway, back on this teacher," Heather said. "Are you going to see him again?"

Deahnna shrugged. "Technically we haven't even seen one another the first time yet. We just happened to both be chaperoning the dance."

"So then we need to formulate a plan to get you two together again."

"Well, I did get his number."

"Well there you go. Have you used it yet?"

"No."

"And you're waiting for what exactly?"

"As I said, he's Brian's teacher. I don't want Brian to be uncomfortable with this."

"Deahnna," Heather said, giving her a scolding look, "Brian is seventeen years old, and I'm sure he has more important things on his mind than worrying about you talking to his teacher. He has a life, unlike you."

Deahnna sighed. "I know what you're saying is right, but it's easier said than done. Especially when you're sitting in the chair I'm sitting in."

"D. I know it's not easy, but you're going to have to start living. Your sanity depends on it, and so does your coochie, because you ain't had none in a while."

Rico said, "Ooh."

Deahnna and everyone else laughed.

"Whatever," Deahnna said, playfully shoving her friend's arm.

Heather waved her hand in front of her nose. "I can smell you from here, girl. It's stale."

More laughter and "ooh's."

"You know what?" Deahnna said. "I can find another boutique."

"Sure you can. But I'm sure they won't be styling you for free." Heather raised her eyebrows.

Deahnna smiled. "OK, you do have me there." She looked at her reflection in the mirror. Heather had hooked her up with a Mary J. Blige shoulder-length cut with blond highlights. Heather had never been the brightest student in school, but if there was one thing she could always do, and do well, it was hair, and the proof showed. "My hair looks good, girl."

"Of course it does. I only do good work. Now let me walk you out of here."

Deahnna rose from the chair, slipped on her jacket, kissed Rico good-bye on his cheek, and followed Heather out of the shop as she zipped up her jacket.

"Damn, it's freezing out here," Deahnna said, shivering.

"Mm-hmm," Heather agreed. "That's why you need to get to that school and snag that man so that you have someone to keep you warm at night."

"You act like I'm desperate."

"Not desperate, girl. You're just in need of some tune-ups. Why do you think I look so good? Because I hit the gym every damn day? Hell to the no! I look this good because I get my oil and battery checked every couple of days, that's why."

Laughing, Deahnna asked, "So how are you and Ivan doing?"

"Lovely," Heather answered. "My Ivan is a man and a sweetheart."

"You are lucky, girl."

Heather put up her hand and flashed her diamond engagement ring. "Don't I know it," she said, smiling and lighting up a cigarette.

"I thought you quit."

"Quitting's for losers. And I ain't no loser."

"You need to quit."

"You quit your part-time job yet?" Heather asked, looking at her intensely.

Deahnna frowned. "Not yet. I want to, but can't afford to do that yet."

Heather raised her eyebrows and shook her head disapprovingly. "Well, when you do, I'll give up the Newports." She dropped the barely smoked butt to the ground. "Girl, I need to get back inside because I'm freezing my little ass off. Besides, you know I can't leave my clients alone with Rico for too long."

"Don't worry. Everyone knows not to pay him any mind."

"Yeah, I know. But his motor mouth can get on your nerves sometimes."

"And you love him regardless."

"Yes, I do love my manly brother. Anyway, call me after you get your date planned with your teacher. And stop by C-Town and pick up an apple before you go see him. Get some bonus points."

"Whatever."

Heather laughed, and then kissed Deahnna on her cheek and rushed back inside.

Deahnna smiled, and then wrapped her arms around herself and headed down Jamaica Avenue. As she did, she thought about when she was going to get up the nerve to call Jawan.

9

"Yo, this better be mad important," Brian said as Will opened the door. "Carla's mom ain't home. I could be chillin' right now."

Will shrugged. "Yo, don't be mad at me, son. I didn't call for this."

Brian frowned. He didn't want to be there. Not only because Carla's mother would be gone for a few hours, but more so because he really didn't want to talk business. The three-man cartel's luck was running out. Brian could feel it in his bones. They'd been lucky with the Laundromat. Lucky that neither Patel nor his wife had been seriously injured. Lucky that Will hadn't said more than he had. And they'd been lucky that nothing further had escalated between Will and Tyrel.

But Brian knew that luck wouldn't be on their side much longer. He'd been tempted to say he couldn't make the meeting, but as badly as he wanted to, he'd never backed out on his boys. So there he was. Reluctantly, with a churning in the pit of his stomach.

He stepped past Will and walked into the living room, where Tyrel was sitting on the couch next to Will's little brother, Marcus, playing *Madden NFL* on the Xbox 360. "What up, son," he said to Tyrel as he sat down beside Marcus.

"Sup," Tyrel said, his jaw hard, his eyes focused intensely on the flat screen. His body was rigid as his fingers furiously worked the buttons and control stick on the game's controller. By the look in his eyes, the baring of his teeth, and the smile plastered on Marcus's face, it was obvious that Tyrel wasn't having a good game.

"Come on, nigga!" Tyrel said, shoving Marcus with his elbow. "Stop fuckin' cheatin'."

"Man, I ain't cheatin'," Marcus said, his voice giddy.

"Whatever, nigga. There ain't no way you could run that bullshit-ass play three times in a row and keep getting twenty yards every ma'fuckin' time without cheatin'."

Marcus laughed. "Maybe you just need to practice."

Tyrel shoved Marcus again. "Whatever, nigga."

Brian exhaled as his thoughts went to Carla. He really was trying to spend more time with her. "Yo, son, put that shit on pause. Let's talk and get it over with."

"Nigga, don't you see I'm tryin' to keep from getting embarrassed?"

"I'm just sayin'," Brian countered. "Carla's mom ain't home."

"Nigga, just chill. Carla's pussy ain't runnin' nowhere."

"Yo," Will said from a chair beside Brian. "Watch the language, son."

Tyrel looked over at him. He said, "Nigga, please," and then focused back on the game.

Brian shook his head and folded his arms across his chest. He wanted to protest again, but knew there was no point to it. He looked over at Will, who looked at him and shrugged again.

Brian looked at the television screen. Tyrel was playing as the Eagles, using Michael Vick as quarterback, while Marcus played as the New York Giants. Marcus had a two-touchdown lead and had the ball on Tyrel's twenty-yard line. He hiked the ball, faked a run to the right, rolled out of the pocket to the left, avoided a rush from the defense, and threw a bullet toward the back of the end zone for another touchdown.

"Goddamn!" Tyrel yelled, slamming the controller down to the carpeted floor. "Don't tell me your ass ain't cheatin', nigga."

Marcus laughed. "I told you, you need to practice, nigga."

"Man, fuck you!" Tyrel stood up and looked at Will. "Your li'l brother's a fuckin' cheater, son."

Will raised his eyebrows. "Yo, he lives and breathes *Madden*."

"Whatever, nigga." He looked down at Marcus. "I'ma get your sister to come and beat your ass like she did in boxing."

"Nah, nigga," Tyrel said, laughing. "You just need to practice."

Brian and Will both laughed as Marcus pouted. Tyrel slapped Marcus heavily in the back of his head, prompting an "ow" from the twelve-year-old.

Tyrel looked at Brian. "You ready now, son."

"Been," Brian said, standing up.

Tyrel walked off to Will's room with Brian and Will in tow. When they got to the room, Will closed the door behind them, while Tyrel sat down on his bed. "Fuckin' cheatin'-ass nigga," he said, still fuming.

"Yo, man, it's just a game," Will said.

"Fuck that game and fuck you and your brother," Tyrel said.

Brian laughed.

"Shit ain't funny," Tyrel said, glaring at him.

Brian put his hand on his stomach. "Yeah, it is," he said, laughing harder.

Tyrel gave him a hard look, and then, seconds later, joined him in laughter. "Fuckin' kids," he said. "All they do is play that shit. I ain't playin' wit' his ass no more."

The three of them laughed hard for a few more seconds, until Tyrel said, "A'ight, we got business to talk about."

Brian and Will stopped laughing immediately.

"What's up?" Brian asked, taking a seat in a chair.

"We about to be paid," Tyrel said.

"Didn't you say that about the Laundromat?" Will asked.

Tyrel gave him a deathly stare that gave Brian the chills. "Nigga," he said, his voice low and taut, "do yourself a favor and don't bring that shit up again."

Even though he'd moved on since that night, it was obvious that Will's actions still left a bitter taste in his mouth. Will gave a nod and didn't say anything else.

"Anyway," Tyrel continued, "the Laundromat wasn't what it was supposed to be, but we still got some cheddar for the night. But now I'm talking about coming off with some real money."

"How?" Will asked.

Brian frowned. He had no interest in how.

"Check cashing," Tyrel said with a sinister smile.

"Check cashing?" Will asked. "You talking about hittin' Old Man Blackwell's joint?"

"Hell yeah, nigga," Tyrel said.

Brian sat forward in his seat. "Yo, Blackwell is like everyone's grandfather around here. We can't fuck with his spot. He looks out for all of us around here."

"Fuck that shit, son," Tyrel said. "He got mad dough in there. We could roll outta there wit' at least sixty thousand easily."

"No shit," Will said with a gleam in his eyes.

Brian shook his head. "Yo, son, I don't care how much money we could pull in, we ain't hittin' Blackwell's spot."

Tyrel looked at Brian with a tight jaw. "What you mean *we* ain't hittin' his spot? What, you the leader now, nigga? You the coach calling all the plays now?"

"It's not about me tryin' to be the leader, Ty. All I'm sayin' is Old Man Blackwell's always looked out for us ever since we were kids. He's always been fair and he's always shown us respect. He don't deserve to be disrespected like that. At least, not by us."

Tyrel sucked his teeth and raised the corner of his mouth while cocking an eyebrow. "Fuck that shit, nigga. Is Blackwell puttin' money in your pocket?" He looked at Will. "Is that nigga payin' your bills, son?"

Will shook his head.

"Shit." He pounded his right fist into his left palm. "This is about survival, son. Old Man Blackwell ain't starvin' and he sure ain't gonna fuckin' die."

"Yo," Brian said, his fists clenched. "I hear what you're sayin', but we can't hit his spot."

"Fuck that, nigga. For thirtysome Gs or more, I'll hit any ma'fuckin' body."

"Yo," Will cut in. "You really think we could pull that much?"

Tyrel turned to him. "Nigga, everyone be cashin' their shit over there."

"What about security though?"

"Big Mike already checked the shit out. Blackwell ain't got but one security camera, and that reformed cokehead, Rich, workin' wit' him. There ain't no security to worry about. All we gotta do is roll in, keep our fuckin' mouths closed," he said, staring hard at Will, "and do what the fuck we need to do and then roll out."

Brian shook his head emphatically. "Nah, man, we can't do it. Blackwell don't deserve that. Not from us."

"Nigga, what the fuck is your problem?" Tyrel snapped. "Did you not hear me say how much we can pull? What, you suddenly get rich and don't need the money?"

"Yo, Brian," Will said, looking at him. "I hear what you're saying. I respect and like Old Man Blackwell too, but . . . shit is rough out here. I can bust my ass all I want at work, but I won't ever see that kind of cash. And I need it, son. I got Marcus and Charmaine to think about."

"I feel you, Will," Brian said, understanding his dilemma. "But that shit ain't right."

Tyrel stood up. "Nigga, what ain't right is you willin' to pass up on some real cheese."

"You gotta draw the line somewhere, son."

"So, what, you sayin' that you bailin' out on your niggas?"

Brian shook his head. "Nah, I ain't sayin' that."

"So then you in."

Brian gritted his teeth and exhaled a heavy breath. "I . . . I can't do it, son."

"So then you bailin' out on your niggas."

Brian frowned. "Man—"

"Yo, which is it, son?" Tyrel cut in. "You either in or out. If you in, cool. But if you out, then you bailin' on us."

Brian rose from the bed. "Why it gotta be me bailin' on you, Ty?"

"Because that's what it is. We a three-man cartel, son."

"I know. Shit," Brian said, frustrated at the predicament he was in.

"So are you in or not?" Tyrel asked.

"Yeah, man," Will added. "Are you down?"

Brian looked over at him. "It's that easy, Will?" he asked.

Will shrugged. "I got my li'l brother and sister to look after."

"And what if something goes wrong, Will? What're Marcus and Charmaine gonna do if you're not around?"

"Ain't nothin' gonna happen, nigga," Tyrel said. "Brian, man, why you being such a bitch about this?"

Brian flared his nostrils, took a breath, held it for a second, and then exhaled. He looked from Will's pleading gaze to Tyrel's cold one.

His boys or Old Man Blackwell.

A man who'd known him since he was two. A man who used to lend him money for pizza when his mother had none. A man who always used to ask about his grades, who always seemed to be concerned as to what he wanted out of his life, and whether or not he was on the right path.

Old Man Blackwell or his boys.

Boys who knew him better than anyone. Boys who'd been with him through thick and thin. Boys who would do anything for him. Go to war for him. Boys who would never choose or put anyone else above him.

Old Man Blackwell or his boys.

Brian shook his head again. "I . . . I gotta think, son," he said, his voice low.

"Think?" Tyrel said. By the tone in his voice, it was obvious that he'd expected a different answer. Had it been any other place, as much as he didn't want to do it, Brian would most likely have given the answer Tyrel wanted to hear. But they were talking about hitting Old Man Blackwell's place, and, whether they liked it or not, the decision wasn't an easy one to make. "Are you for real, son?"

"Yeah, man," Brian said. "I'm for real. I need to think about it."

Tyrel laughed, though it was hardly one filled with amusement. "Can you believe this nigga, Will? He has to think about sellin' his boys out. That's some fucked-up shit, right?"

Will looked at Brian and frowned, but remained silent.

"Yo, fuck you, Ty. I ain't sellin' nobody out."

Tyrel stepped toward Brian. Not stopping until his face was inches away from Brian's. "No, fuck *you*, nigga," he said, his tone acerbic. "You a fuckin' bitch ass, son," he spat.

Brian's heart beat heavily as he closed fists at his sides. Fighting was nothing to him, but he'd never fought his boy. "Yo, Ty, back down, son."

"Or what, nigga?" Ty challenged, decreasing the inches between them.

"Ty," Brian said, his heart beating faster, "I ain't tryin' to beef with you, a'ight? Just step down."

"Fuck you, nigga. I step down for nobody."

Brian ground his teeth together, and flared his nostrils. He'd known only bad things were coming. He should have just stayed with Carla.

He looked at Tyrel. They'd had each other's backs so many times before in the past, yet now here they were, inches and seconds away from going toe-to-toe. Tyrel was the thicker and more relentless of the two, but Brian was the better fighter.

They stared.

Barely breathed.

Seconds passed.

Brian could feel the point of no return coming. The moment when the first punch would be thrown and nothing would ever be the same again. He felt it in the tips of his fingers, along the hairs on the back of his neck.

He closed his fists tighter, his nails digging into the palm of his hands. He'd hit first. But before he could, Will sprang up and backed them both up with his hands.

"Yo, come on. Y'all niggas need to chill."

Tyrel glared at Brian over Will's shoulder. "You want some, nigga?"

"Bring it, son," Brian answered, trying to rush forward.

"Come on," Will said, pushing them both back again. He looked at Brian. "Yo, B, go home, son. Go home and think or do whatever, a'ight?"

"Yeah, nigga," Tyrel said. "Go home before you get

hurt."

Brian tried to rush forward.

Will pushed hard against his chest. "Yo, B, Ty. Come on. Y'all are boys!"

"Boys don't sell one another out," Tyrel said.

"Ain't nobody sellin' you out, man!"

Brian worked his jaw.

Tyrel flexed his chest.

They were two rams on the verge of butting horns.

"Marcus, get off! Ow! *Will!*"

Will, Tyrel, and Brian looked toward the door. On the other side, Charmaine was crying and yelling at Marcus, and screaming for Will.

Brian let out the breath he'd been holding. Although he didn't want it to happen, he knew that nothing could happen between him and Tyrel. At least not there. He turned and looked back to Tyrel, who still had his eyes locked on him. *My boy,* he thought.

This wasn't supposed to be happening.

Brian unclenched his fists, let his shoulders drop, and without a word, walked out of the room and headed back to Carla's. He was stressed, and only she could diffuse the bomb ticking inside of him.

10

Deahnna couldn't believe she was about to do what she was about to do. It was a big step. One she hadn't thought she'd ever take. At least, not again. Not since she'd all but shut herself down. She never wanted to hurt again, and although she'd only had two negative experiences, the two that she did have had been more than enough for her to decide that she never wanted to venture down the path of pain and unhappiness again. Therefore, relationships, and even the thought of them, were off-limits.

The decision had left her lonely at times, but looking at the big picture, loneliness was far better than the emotional turmoil she'd had to deal with.

But now her toes were teetering on the edge of a cliff, and in seconds, if she actually went through with it, she was going to freefall to an unknown landing that for so long she'd assumed could only be disastrous.

If she went through with it.

Pressing the last digit on her cell phone that would connect her phone to Jawan White's.

The palms of her hands were slick with perspiration. She took a breath as her heart thumped beneath her chest. "This is ridiculous," she said to herself. "It's just a phone call." She exhaled and wiped her palms on the sweats she was wearing.

Just a phone call.

"That's all it is."

She pressed the last digit and immediately freaked out.

What if the call went well? What if the conversation went as smoothly as it had in the gymnasium? What if the call ended with plans for a date? And what if the date went well and led to a second one? And if the second one led to a third, and that third led to an eventual relationship, what then? He would know things, but he wouldn't know everything, because he couldn't. So, really, what was the point to all of this? *Why set yourself up for failure, for heartache? Chemistry or not, does this really make any sense at all?*

She hit the end button, canceling the call, and put the phone down on the bed beside her. "Stupid," she said. "Just stupid. You know you can't do this. You know you couldn't tell him everything about you. Dammit. What were you thinking?" She felt a tear snake from the corner of her eye, and slammed her hand down on her mattress. "Dammit," she whispered again. "Dammit, Terrance!"

Had she just never let him touch her, she wouldn't be going through this right now. Had she just never fallen for his bullshit and just waited like she was supposed to. She was only sixteen, for Christ's sake! All she had to do was wait for the right guy, the right time. She wouldn't have to deal with the stress, the anxiety. She wouldn't be a prisoner, locked away from the freedom of love. The freedom she'd seen so many others experience and treasure. Her decision would be easy. The phone call would simply be . . .

She shook her head and frowned as reality hit her.

Without Terrance and without her naivety, the phone call she'd just disconnected would have been nonexistent. And if the call were nonexistent, so too would be her son, and she just didn't know life without her baby.

She looked down at her phone. Good, bad, and ugly, all things in life happened for a reason. The emotional scarring was hard to deal with and accept at times, but Brian's existence made it all worth it. "Just a phone call," she said. "Dammit, Deahnna, just admit it. You felt it."

She wiped her teary streak away with the back of her hand, and then reached out to grab her phone, when The Jackson 5's song, "I'll Be There" suddenly pierced the silence, causing her heart to skip a beat. She grabbed her phone and looked at the caller ID. Brian wasn't home, and she anticipated that it would be him.

But it wasn't.

Deahnna froze as she looked at the screen and the phone number lit up in yellow. She was familiar with the number, but only because she'd just dialed it seconds ago.

She stared at the phone in her hand, listening to Michael Jackson at nine years old outsing most current-day singers she knew. The phone felt hot in her palm. Almost electric.

Chemistry, she thought.

It was there. She knew it.

"Put it down," she whispered. And then she hit the talk button and put the phone against her ear. "He . . ." She paused, cleared a frog from her throat, and said again, "Hello?"

"Uh, hello. Someone just called me from this number," Jawan said on the other end, caution in his voice.

"Hi, Jawan, it . . . it's me, Deahnna Moore. Brian Moore's mother. We met at the school dance."

The tone in Jawan's voice picked up immediately as he said, "Hey, Deahnna! I'm sorry I didn't recognize your voice."

"Yeah. I, uh, had something in my throat."

"Are you OK?"

"Yes. I'm fine."

"Good. So why did you hang up?"

"I'm sorry. I got another call just as I was calling you that I had to take."

"Oh. Well, do you need me to let you go?"

"No, no. I'm . . . my call is finished."

"OK. Good. So how have you been?"

Deahnna smiled at the sincerity in his voice. "I've been good. Had a busy rest of the weekend, and then work today, and a hair appointment to fix myself up right afterward. Kind of been nonstop since we've spoken."

"I see that. So, a hair appointment to fix yourself up?"

"Yeah. I was looking a little raggedy."

"Really? From where I was standing, you were looking far from raggedy," he said, the tone in his voice dipping to a low, seductive growl that made bumps rise along Deahnna's arms.

"It was dark in the gym," she said, her cheeks feeling warm. "You didn't really get a good look."

"Oh, trust me, I got a very good look."

Deahnna's smile widened, and she was glad she wasn't standing in front of him having this conversation. She cleared her throat. "So, I had a good time Friday night."

"So did I," Jawan replied.

Deahnna chuckled. "Believe it or not, it was actually one of the best nights out that I've had in a long while."

"Hmm," Jawan said. "And it wasn't even a date."

Just imagine if it were, Deahnna thought. "So, are you busy?" she asked.

"Not extremely. I'm just here at the school grading some papers."

Deahnna looked at the time on her alarm clock sitting on her night table. It was nearing seven o'clock. "Do you always work this late?"

"More than I like to. I occasionally take work home, but I try to leave that time for myself. It helps keep me sane, you know."

"Yeah," Deahnna agreed. There was a brief moment of silence, but the silence didn't feel awkward. Instead, it just felt . . . natural. Felt as though they could sit together in silence and everything would be just fine. "So," she said after another couple of seconds. "How is Grady?"

During their conversation at the dance, he'd mentioned his feline companion.

"You remembered his name. I'm impressed."

"Well, I was paying attention."

"I see that." Jawan laughed. "Grady is loving life as a bachelor."

"Mm-hmm. I see. So the bachelor life is where it's at, huh?"

"For Grady it is."

"Oh, come on. And it's not for you?"

"Trust me, the bachelor life is overrated."

"I bet a lot of guys would beg to differ on that."

"Guess I'm just not like a lot of guys," Jawan replied, his voice confident.

Deahnna raised her eyebrows. *No, you're not,* she thought.

"I'm actually thinking about converting Grady, though," Jawan said.

"Converting him?"

"Yeah. I'm thinking about finding him a little kitty to keep him company."

"Really? Why?"

"Grady's a great cat, but he has a tendency to disturb my sleep, especially in the morning. I figure with a lady friend in his life, he could leave me alone."

Deahnna laughed. "Aren't you worried about becoming a grandfather?"

"Nah. I'll just put him out if that happens."

"That's mean."

"Hey, if he wants to act like a man, then he'll have to

do what a man's supposed to do and support his family. I told him that too."

Deahnna laughed again, something she found very easy to do with him. "You better be nice to Grady, or I'll have to come over there and rescue him, and then report you to the humane society."

"You come over here?" Jawan said. "Hold on. Let me go and hang him by his tail really quick."

More laughter from Deahnna as Jawan called out his pet's name.

"You're just mean," she said, chuckling.

"So, you're coming over then?"

"Ha-ha. Not tonight."

"Sorry, Grady. Looks like we'll have to postpone the torture to, say, Friday night?"

Deahnna smiled. *Very, very smooth*, she thought. "Are you asking me out, Mr. White?" she asked, surprised at the playfulness in her voice.

"I'm just saying . . . Friday night would be a good night to torture Grady."

"In that case, I guess I need to make sure that night is free for me to rescue him, huh?"

"You don't have to. But I can't promise that Grady would make it through the night."

"You're a sick, sick man," Deahnna said.

Jawan laughed. "Tell you what: why don't I save the torture for another night, and maybe on Friday we can do a movie or something?"

"Hmm . . ."

"Torture or a movie. It's up to you."

"You drive a hard bargain," Deahnna said.

"Hey, I'm just giving you options."

Deahnna laughed and shook her head. "OK, sicko, if I must choose . . . let's go with the movie."

"OK. Anything in particular that you want to see?"

"I'm open for anything. You pick."

"*OK,*" Jawan said. "*Debbie Does Dallas* it is."

"Ha-ha. Nice try."

Jawan laughed. "Hey, you said you're open for anything."

"Not that open."

"OK, OK. I'll skip that one for now and pick something a little lighter for you."

"Mm-hmm."

"So, Friday at seven?"

"Seven is fine with me."

"OK. What's your address?"

"Tell you what: why don't I meet you at the school?"

"Ah. I take it you don't want Brian to know?"

"Well, you are his teacher. It might be a little awkward for him."

"Hmm. OK. I'll concede."

"Thank you."

"No problem."

Another few moments of comfortable silence passed before Jawan said, "Well, I don't want to go, but I have papers to finish grading."

"I understand. Well, it was very nice talking to you again."

"Yes, it was," Jawan agreed.

"Don't kill Grady tonight."

"On my honor, I promise not to touch a hair on his head until you can come and save his hide."

Deahnna smiled, and felt her cheeks grow warm again. "OK."

"I'll see you Friday, then."

"OK. Good night, Jawan."

"Good night, Deahnna."

Deahnna ended the call, and the smile that was spread across her face grew wider. She lay back against her headboard, took a breath, and let it out slowly.

She had a date.

She was still uncertain about the landing, but she never imagined freefalling could feel this good.

11

She said yes.

Jawan smiled, and drew a red line through a wrong answer on an exam paper he was grading.

Since he'd given Deahnna his cell number, every time his cell phone rang, Jawan had looked at it with eager anticipation, hoping it would be her. There'd been an instant chemistry between them, and his hope was that she'd felt it too, thereby prompting her to call him the next day, even though he knew the chances of that were slim because rarely did anyone ever call the very next day or, sometimes, even the day after that. But she'd said she'd been on the go all weekend, and Jawan could tell by the tone in her voice that she'd felt the connection too. He had no doubt that had her days not been so hectic, he would have heard from her sooner.

He smiled again, but then quickly frowned as he drew red lines through another two wrong answers. It was Eduardo's paper. His shoulders dropped a bit as he let out a breath filled with disappointment. No matter how hard he tried, he just couldn't seem to convince Eduardo that life didn't end after high school. That he could be more than just the class clown.

It was a battle he and many other teachers were fighting every day across the country, and while there were victories, there were just far too many losses. Far too many kids with defeatist attitudes, who teachers, despite their best efforts, just could not reach. Eduardo had the potential to be like LaKeisha and Brian, and a few other students he had, but in Eduardo's mind, the payoff of college and beyond just wasn't worth the effort.

Jawan frowned, wrote a large D at the top of Eduardo's test, and grabbed another exam to grade, while putting his mind back on Deahnna Moore.

She'd said yes.

He hadn't necessarily intended on asking her out so quickly, but their conversation had been so natural, so easy, and so free, that popping the question just seemed like the logical thing to do.

And she'd said yes.

Jawan smiled as he quickly ran through LaKeisha's exam. As was always the case, she'd aced it. He gave her an A and then grabbed one of two papers he had left. This one belonged to Brian. As he did, his cell phone rang. He looked at it, hoping it would be Deahnna again. But it wasn't, and the call was no less disappointing.

"What's up, fool!" he said, answering.

"JawanaMan. What's up, dude!"

Jawan smiled. When the ridiculous movie came out years ago, his cousin, Nick, automatically gave him the moniker.

Nick had moved from New York to Los Angeles to pursue his dream of becoming an Academy Award–winning actor. He wanted to be the next Denzel and be in an ungodly amount of movies like Samuel L. Jackson. He'd taken countless acting classes to refine and develop his craft, and had performed in numerous off-Broadway roles before making the leap to LA.

But his road to getting his star on the Hollywood Walk of Fame had taken a detour when he was approached at the gym one day and offered a payment of $5,000 to star in a film that was being shot the following day. Living life as a struggling and starving actor, the $5,000 had been just the thing Nick had needed, as his rent was two months overdue, his refrigerator and cupboards were anorexic, and he was sure his Jeep was days away from being repossessed. He did the job the next day, received the cash as promised, and before his head had hit the pillow that night, he had four more acting gigs lined up. Nick still hoped to land an Oscar, or at least a role that would propel him toward receiving one, but until then, he was content being a leading man in the adult film industry.

"What's up, cuz?" Jawan said, putting his pen down.

"Not much, dude. Just got a break between shots, and I wanted to give you a shout about something before I got back to work."

"Work? What you do is work?"

"Shee-it, dude. You have no idea. Hittin' pussy for a living ain't all it's cracked up to be."

"Yeah. OK."

"I'm serious, dude. Some days I can't even get my shit up for the scenes."

"Really?"

"Man, if it weren't for the special handlers we have on set . . ." Nick paused and blew out a breath. "It looks glamorous on the TV screen, dude, but, trust me, it's grueling work."

"Damn, Nick. If it's that tough, then why don't you get out of the business and try to hit the mainstream?"

Nick sucked his teeth. "Dude, unless your name is Denzel, Will, Samuel, or maybe Don, Hollywood ain't tryin' to give a brotha a real role. And they most certainly are not going to pay me what I'm making now. Shit, grueling work or not, fucking pussy is a lucrative profession."

Jawan laughed. "Yeah, I know it is."

"You could be collecting this green too, dude. I told you I have mad movies for you to star in."

Jawan shook his head and leaned back in his chair. "Thanks, but I'll pass. I don't think that would be a good example for the kids. I'll just leave it to you professionals."

"Shit, dude, if you know how to bang a chick, then you're already a pro."

Jawan laughed again. "Thanks, but I'm happy to be a spectator every now and then, catching it on Cinemax."

"Cinemax?" Nick said. "Shit. That's baby stuff."

"Well, it's sufficient for most people."

"Yeah, OK. Anyway, dude, I wanted to ask you something."

"What's up?"

"Will you be one of the groomsmen in my wedding?"

Jawan sat up in his seat. "Wedding? What? Hold up. Something's wrong with my cell, because it sounded like you were telling me that you're getting married. That's not what you were saying, was it?"

Nick laughed. "Yeah, dude. I'm getting married."

Jawan's turn to say, "Shee-it. Nick the Dick is getting married. The world is coming to an end. So who is the, um, lucky woman? And does she know what you do for a living?"

"Her name is Cheryl Hannah, although you might know her as Mylie Stylus."

Mylie Stylus. Behind Jenna Jameson and a few others, she was one of the bigger female stars in the porn industry. Her movies were well known.

"For real?"

"Yeah, dude. We've done a couple of movies together, and unlike with all of the other people we worked with, when we kissed and fucked, it was real, because we had a real connection. We started dating exclusively about six months ago, and I just popped the question last night."

"Damn, cuz. Well, congrats."

"Thanks, dude. It was unexpected, but it's real and it feels good being with her."

"Cool. But I have to ask: with her becoming your wife, does that change how you feel about other guys having sex with her?"

"Hell yeah, it does," Nick exclaimed. "And it's changed for her too."

"So, how are you two going to deal with that? I mean, that's what your profession is all about."

"We've already talked to our agents and all the directors we work with. We reworked our contracts to state that the only kind of sex we're going to have with the opposite sex will be oral. When it comes to fucking, we'll be fucking each other exclusively."

"Oh. OK. I guess that's a good compromise," Jawan said, cocking an eyebrow.

"Yeah. Oral ain't shit but sucking and licking. There's nothing personal about it."

"OK," Jawan said, not particularly buying the logic.

"So anyway, dude, we're getting married in two months and I want you to be a groomsman. I would have had you be the best man, but I had to reserve that for her dad, since it was on his film set that I first met her."

"Her dad?"

"Yeah. He's a director."

"Damn."

"All you need is a plane ticket, dude. Then you can come and join the family and get paid."

"Hmm. Intriguing, but, again, I'll respectfully pass."

Nick laughed. "So what's up, JawanaMan. You my groomsman or what?"

"Of course."

"Cool. The wedding's gonna be out here, but my boy Tracy's gonna throw a bachelor party for me in NYC in about a month, so I'll see you before then. And I know you're not missing that."

"Cool. And definitely not."

"Good stuff. So anyway, how are things on your end? Still teaching at Lane?"

"Yeah. Still here."

"Nice. What about females? You get over your ex's ass yet and start living again?"

Jawan smiled as an image of Deahnna flashed in his mind. "Yeah, man. I did. I actually met someone."

"Oh yeah? About damn time. So who is she and where did you meet. Was it at the library? I hear they're freakier than the chicks you meet in church."

Jawan broke out in laughter. "I didn't meet her at the library, but I did meet her at the school. Well, the school dance."

"Really? She's a teacher?"

"The mother of one of my students, actually."

"Word?"

"Yeah. We were both chaperoning the dance last Friday. We kind of hit it off there. We're going out this Friday night."

"Good stuff, dude. Sounds like it could be something."

Jawan raised his brow. "Definitely could be."

"Cool. Well, if she's still around when the wedding comes, make sure you bring her."

"Will do."

"All right, dude. They're calling me over. I'm getting a blowjob from two midget females."

Jawan shook his head. "You're crazy, man."

"Tell Scorsese to cast me in his next blockbuster and to pay me what Will is getting, and I'll leave this all behind. Until then, I'm busting a nut and getting paid."

"OK, cuz," Jawan said, wiping tears from the corners of his eyes as he laughed. "Go and suffer through it."

"All right. I'll e-mail you info about the bachelor party and all of the wedding details in a couple of days."

"OK, man."

His cousin ended the call. Jawan hit the end button, put his cell down, and shook his head with a smile. "Married," he said. "Craziness."

He picked up his red pen, grabbed Brian's test paper, and was prepared to write an A across the top when he noticed something odd. Brian had answered the first question incorrectly. Jawan marked a red line through it, and then went to the second question, and was surprised to see that it too was wrong. He went through the rest of the paper, and when he was finished, he wrote a C- across the top.

Something wasn't right.

He knew Brian knew the answers to the questions, because he'd answered almost all of them during class discussions on different days.

Something was definitely not right.

Had his wrong answers been in retaliation for the conversation Jawan had had with him after class? Would he sabotage his grade in order to make Jawan leave his mother alone?

Jawan shook his head.

Brian wasn't that stupid. He wasn't that irresponsible.

Something else had to be behind the C-.

Jawan gathered all of the exams, putting Brian's at the top. He would have a talk with his student to find out what was going on. Brian had too much potential for something like this to be ignored. Besides, he'd meant what he'd said to Nick. Something was there with Deahnna.

If he played his cards right and the stars remained aligned, then that something could lead to him and Brian being a whole lot closer.

12

Deahnna cried.

She was doing what she had to do. Sacrificing to hold things down. Sacrificing to keep a roof over her head. Sacrificing to put food on the table, to keep the utilities on.

Her sanity.

Tiny bits of her soul.

Sacrificing.

Three nights a week. Four hours at a time. Twelve hours total. Deahnna did what she never imagined she would ever do or, for that matter, ever have to do. But life's circumstances dictated the tough, heart-wrenching decision she'd had to make, and so on Thursday, Friday, and Saturday nights, she left the peace and comfort of her home, hopped on the J train, and took a thirty-minute, solitary commute to a place where the only thing she didn't reveal was her name.

Deahnna cried.

While everyone stared but didn't see.

Her tears came down torrentially. Droplets as heavy as lead marbles. As cold as ice. Hard, fast, unrelenting. Unforgiving.

She cried.

While she worked her hips seductively. While she gripped a metal pole with one hand and caressed her breast with the other. While Ginuwine's classic, erotically-charged song, "Pony," played from speakers all around her. While strangers, both familiar and unfamiliar, watched her intensely with their mouths open, their hands loosely holding on to dollar bills, or sitting heavily in their crotches.

She cried.

On the inside. Where no one ever saw.

Deahnna worked her body like a snake, going down to her knees, the metal pole sitting in the middle of her back. Her eyes stared through the men and women watching her. They all assumed she was staring at them. That was never the case. Deahnna never noticed anyone.

She got down on her hands and knees and began to crawl slowly toward the front of the stage that she commanded. She licked her lips as though they were coated with honey. She bit down on her bottom lip as if squirming around on the laminated flooring was the best sex she'd ever had. She smiled, and blew kisses to spectators who tossed dollar bills at her.

Her performance was always waited for with eager anticipation. She was the seductress who wore a mask like Zorro. Deahnna sexed the air around her to the song's hypnotic rhythm, making everyone yearn to be with her, to touch her, to kiss her, to move inside of her.

She cried as she sacrificed her self-respect for the extra cash that her full-time job didn't give her. But she continued to move, to put on her show, to entice everyone to make their hard-earned money hers, until the song came to a merciful end.

She gathered the many dollar bills lying around her on the stage as people applauded and the club's owner praised the "big ass" and "beautiful tits" she had, and then quickly shuffled off of the stage, going to the dressing rooms where two other dancers waited their turn.

She sat down, and no longer able to keep the tears buried deep, she covered her face with her hands and let them overflow and cascade down her cheeks.

"Deahnna, what's wrong, girl?"

Deahnna looked up as a small hand lay on her shoulder. One of the other dancers, Regina Tatum, stood beside her, looking down at her with a concerned frown. Regina was the senior dancer in the club. Senior meaning her age. Forty-five, with weathered skin tinged by age spots, and D-cups that hung just a little too low. A pockmarked face that looked weighted down by makeup. Regina had been stripping for close to twenty years. From LA to Vegas. From Vegas to Chicago. Chi-town to the Big Apple. She'd traveled long and she'd traveled hard. She really had no right being on the stage, but she gave lap dances that drew lines, and she also gave the club's owner head that made him moan like a cat in heat. Whether she belonged or not, as long as the lines and the owner continued to come, she could dance for as long as she wanted to.

Deahnna sniffled, reached for a tissue, and wiped her eyes. "Nothing," she said. "I'm fine."

"OK," Regina said in a "yeah, right" tone. "Whatever you say, honey."

"Really," Deahnna said. "I just have some things I'm dealing with, but I'm OK."

"Honey, we're all dealing with shit by being here, so stop trying to be tough and just talk to me."

Deahnna smiled. For the most part she got along with all of the dancers in the club, but she'd developed an especially close bond with Regina. She frowned as Regina looked at her sympathetically. After a few seconds, she frowned and said, "I hate doing this job."

Regina raised her eyebrows. "Don't we all, honey."

"I never thought I would ever have to do something like this."

"Believe me, I never planned on making this a career. I wanted to be a doctor or a lawyer. But I followed the wrong crowd when I was younger, and got caught up in things that took my dreams away."

Deahnna shook her head and thought about Brian. If he ever found out what her real part-time job was . . . And then there was Jawan. The man who'd come in like a white knight. If he ever knew . . .

"I have to get out of this, Regina. But life is just so damned hard and unfair."

"I know, honey," Regina said, her voice soft.

Deahanna wiped her eyes with the tissue again. "I . . . I have to find something else." She'd looked for other part-time jobs, but the problem was that in order to make what she made at the club, she'd have to put in a lot more hours. She looked at Regina. "I met someone," she said with a smile.

"Really? He doesn't come here, does he? Because let me tell you, those relationships never work."

"No," Deahnna said, shaking her head emphatically. "He's actually a teacher."

"Hmm. I see. He doesn't teach sex ed. Does he?" Regina said with a laugh.

Deahnna laughed too. Something she hadn't done all night. "No. He's an English teacher."

"Sounds nice."

"I have a date with him tomorrow night."

"Good for you, honey."

Deahnna pressed the tissue to her eyes again. "He . . . he knows I work a second job, but he doesn't know what it is. What if he starts asking me about it? I can't tell him what I do. I didn't regret agreeing to the date before, but now I'm really starting to."

Regina squeezed her shoulder. "Honey, you've been here for six months now, and as long as I've known you, you've never talked about a man, which means this guy must be special."

Deahnna smiled and nodded. "He is."

"Well then go out tomorrow night and have a good time, honey."

"And what if he asks about this job?"

"You lie."

"But to establish a relationship based on a lie—"

"Is the smart thing to do right now, honey." Regina looked over her shoulder as applause and whistling erupted from the stage. She looked back to Deahnna. "Looks like I'm on. Listen, trust me on this. Go out and lie about what you do, honey. Tell him that you work for a cleaning company. Go with the flow. Let the relationship get established. When and if you need to tell him about this place, he'll hopefully know you well enough to know that this bullshit is all about doing what you have to do. Not what you want to do."

"I . . . I guess."

Regina leaned over and gave her a kiss on her forehead. "Trust me, honey, let him get to know you. Once he does, if you do have to tell him, he'll know that something like this can't define you. Gotta run. There are pervs and dollar bills waiting."

"OK. Hey. Thanks, Regina."

"Anytime, honey. See you on Saturday. Have details. Especially of the sex."

Deahnna laughed. "I don't think that will be happening. It's only our first date."

"And?" Regina blew her a kiss and left the room, leaving her alone.

Deahnna thought about Jawan. He'd been on her mind since their phone conversation. She'd said that sex wasn't happening, but she couldn't deny that sexual energy had existed between them the night of the dance.

Sex.

It had been awhile since she'd had any, awhile since she'd really even thought about it. But since the night of the dance, she'd definitely had a tingling between her legs.

She'd meant it when she said she didn't think anything would be happening, but in the back of her mind, she couldn't help but think that maybe she should be prepared for the unplanned.

13

Yo . . . sup B . . . You down?

Brian clenched his jaw and deleted the text message he'd just received from Tyrel. He'd gotten numerous messages from Will. This was the first correspondence he'd gotten from Tyrel since their near blowup at Will's house. Brian slid his phone back into his pocket.

Was he down?

To rip off Old Man Blackwell. A man who knew his mother well. A man who'd always given him smiles and respect.

Was he down?

To disrespect Old Man Blackwell in order to respect bonds of a friendship that went back so far he couldn't remember a time without it. Tyrel and Will. The two musketeers in their three-musketeer tandem. One for all and all for one. No blood existed between them, yet to say they weren't brothers just didn't make sense.

Was he down?

Blackwell or his comrades, who struggled to survive in the war of life.

Brian shook his head, dragged his hand down over his face, and exhaled heavily through flared nostrils. He shouldn't have had to make a decision like this.

"Hey, Brian."

Brian looked up. His teacher, Mr. White, was standing in front of him. He'd been so caught up in his thoughts and dilemma that he'd never even noticed his teacher approach him. "Hey, Mr. White," he said, his voice low.

"Do me a favor and hang out after class, OK?"

"I have something to do," Brian said.

"Just give me a few minutes. Maybe fifteen, tops."

Brian opened his mouth to protest, but then closed it. "OK," he mumbled.

His teacher nodded and then walked off. Brian frowned and wondered what his teacher wanted. Hopefully it had nothing to do with his mom.

Despite the fact that Mr. White had insisted he'd had no intentions with his mother, Brian still had his doubts. He'd watched their interaction at the dance from afar. He'd seen the look of interest in his teacher's eyes. He wanted his mother whether he admitted it or not. Although Brian liked and respected, and even trusted to a certain degree, his teacher, that want in his eyes bothered him. He took a breath and let it out slowly. He had enough on his mind as it was. He didn't need any more shit to deal with.

His cell phone buzzed again. Another message. He pulled it out from his pocket, held it beneath his desk, and looked down at it. It was a note from Carla.

My mother had to go into work to cover for someone. I need to talk to you. Come over after school.

Brian texted back: *Talk about what?*

Thirty seconds passed, and then: *Just come over. It's important.*

Too much shit, Brian thought.

He replied, *OK,* and then slid his phone back into his pocket. Fifteen minutes later, the bell rang, letting everyone know that the school day had ended.

While the students rushed out, Brian remained seated. When the room was empty, Mr. White approached him with a paper in his hand. He put the paper down in front of Brian. Brian looked at it. His exam. With a C- on it.

"You want to explain that to me?" his teacher said.

Brian looked at the paper, then at him. "It looks like a C-," he said nonchalantly.

Mr. White nodded. "On your paper," he said. "You want to tell me why?"

"What do you mean why?"

"I know you know the answers to these questions, Brian, yet you answered some incorrectly, and there were a couple that you just didn't answer at all."

Brian raised his brow and shrugged.

"What's going on, Brian? This I-don't-care façade isn't working. I know you. I know you care about your grades."

"Nothing's going on," Brian answered. "I just screwed up. Didn't study properly."

Mr. White frowned and looked at him, his eyes clearly stating that he wasn't buying Brian's bullshit. "Are you in any trouble?"

Brian said, "No."

"What about your mother?"

Brian shook his head. "No."

"Are your boys in trouble?"

"Nah. They're good."

"So then what's the deal? I don't want Cs on your papers to become the norm."

Brian bent the corners of his mouth downward and kept his lips tight as he exhaled. "Nothing's the deal, Mr. White. I just screwed up on the test. That's it. It's not going to become routine."

His teacher looked at him, his eyes still filled with skepticism. "Screwed up, huh?" he said.

"Yeah."

"So I guess that means that I should expect the usual with your next exam."

"Yeah."

His teacher nodded. "And there's nothing going on?

Nothing on your mind? Nothing that you need to talk about?"

Brian grit his teeth and remained silent for a brief moment. He needed to talk to someone, but he was part of a three-man cartel. There was no one he could talk to. He shook his head. "Nothing," he said. "I'm good."

Mr. White nodded again. "OK. I'll take you at your word. I'll see you next Monday."

Brian gave a nod back, then gathered his book bag and rose from his desk. About to walk away, his teacher, who'd gone back to his desk, called out to him.

"Brian, before you go, I just want you to know that if you ever need someone to talk to, I'm here with a closed mouth and an open and nonjudgmental ear."

Brian's heart beat heavily, and for a brief moment he toyed with the idea of opening up. There was a sincerity in his teacher's voice, something reassuring about it that he found trustworthy. He stared at Mr. White as the teacher watched him. *Open up,* he thought. He wanted to, needed to. *But how do you tell someone that you're a thief?*

Brian gave a half smile. "Thanks," he said, and then quickly left the classroom.

14

Fifteen minutes later, Brian was ringing Carla's doorbell.

She wanted to talk about something important. He didn't know what she wanted to talk about, but she'd never wanted to talk about anything important before.

He took a deep breath as he waited for her to open the door, and blew it out slowly.

Will's near screwup at Patel's Laundromat. The decision about Old Man Blackwell's, and the near fight with his best friend. The struggle to remain focused in school. Now Carla wanted to talk about something important. The storm was looming closer. He could feel it.

The door opened.

Carla looked at him for a short second, and then stepped to the side and said, "Come in."

No smile. No hug. No kiss.

Very different from the last time they were together.

Whatever the important topic was, it wasn't going to be good.

Brian said, "Hey," then walked in, giving Carla a quick peck on her lips as he passed by her.

Carla closed the door and then turned toward him. She was wearing a blue New York Giants T-shirt and a pair of gray sweatpants, and had New York Giants slippers on her feet. She loved football and bled New York Giants blue.

Carla was very much a what-you-see-is-what-you-get type of girl. Jeans, sweats, T-shirts—these were the things she preferred to wear. She liked makeup and liked to get her hair done every week, but other than that, she was not the type of female to feel the need to dress to impress all the time. That was one of the things Brian liked about her. She was an around-the-way girl in the truest form. She kept it simple, but was always sexy with it.

Brian looked at her. Used X-ray vision to see the curves he knew very well beneath the clothing. He was there because she wanted to talk about something important, but they had the house to themselves. He couldn't fight the stirring in his black South Pole jeans.

He put his bag down. "You look good," he said, the tone in his voice indicating that he was hoping talking wouldn't be the only thing they would do.

Carla frowned, folded her arms across her chest, and said, "I'm pregnant."

Nothing more.

Brian stopped breathing.

He just stared. His gaze going from Carla's eyes to her stomach.

Pregnant.

That meant there was a baby inside.

Brian stared. Didn't move. Didn't blink. Didn't breathe. Just stared.

"So," Carla said. "Say something."

Brian swallowed saliva that wasn't there, but still didn't move, blink, breathe, or speak.

"Brian," Carla called out. "Brian, say something."

Brian's gaze traveled up from her belly to her eyes. Tears were running from them, and trailing down her cheeks.

He hated to see her cry. He finally breathed, and then said, "Are . . . are you sure?"

Carla nodded and brushed dark brown hair away from her face. "Yeah. The test is positive."

"The test could be wrong."

"I took four of them. They all had the same result."

"Four? What the hell? What made you take the test in the first place?"

"I missed my period last month."

Brian clamped his hand behind his neck. "Last month? Shit. Why are you just now telling me this?"

"I was sick last month with the cold, remember? I didn't know if somehow the cold made me miss it."

"Colds don't affect a fucking period," Brian said louder than he intended.

"I just wanted to be sure, all right?"

"Fuck, Carla! How can you be fuckin' pregnant?"

Carla wiped tears away furiously with the back of her hand as her face grew red. "What do you mean how can I be? Your ass was the one who insisted on us not using any condoms."

Brian dragged his hand down over his face, cursed, and then turned and paced back and forth. "Goddamn," he said, pissed at himself for her all-too-true statement. "This is fucked up, Carla. Real fucked up."

"Don't you think I know that?" Carla snapped back, her tears falling fast. "I wasn't trying to be nobody's mother right now."

Brian sat down on the faux leather sofa. He leaned forward, resting his elbows on his knees, clasped his hands together, bounced on the toes of his right foot, and stared down at the floor.

Pregnant.

"Goddamn, Carla," he said again. "I got enough shit to deal with."

"Well, I'm so glad I added to the shit you have to deal with, because I certainly didn't have any of my own to add to!"

Brian slammed his fists down on the sofa cushions. "Fuck!"

Carla wiped tears away. Said, "So what are we going to do?"

Brian looked up at her. "What do you mean what are we gonna do? We gotta get money together for an abortion. What you think?"

Carla closed her eyes, put her hand over her mouth, and sobbed heavily.

Brian slouched back against the couch and interlocked his fingers on the top of his head.

Pregnant.

He stomped his foot down and cursed out loud again.

Fucking pregnant.

He hated that it invaded his thoughts right now, but his thoughts went to Will, Tyrel, and the answer they were waiting for.

Was he down?

Fifteen minutes ago, his mind, still not completely made up, his answer on its way to being a no. He had to draw the line. Boys or not, he couldn't disrespect Old Man Blackwell. But Carla hadn't sent him a text saying that she needed to talk about something important. She hadn't told him that she was pregnant. Fifteen minutes ago, he hadn't needed money for a goddamned abortion.

"I . . . I'm not getting an abortion," Carla said.

Brian's eyes snapped open. "What?"

Carla shook her head slowly. "I . . . I'm not getting an abortion," she said. "I don't believe in them."

Brian closed his eyes a bit. "What do you mean you don't believe in them?"

Her voice stronger, Carla said, "I'm not getting an abortion. It goes against what I believe."

Brian sat forward. "I'm not trying to be a father right now, Carla!"

"Like I said, Brian, I'm not exactly looking to be a mother either, but—"

"But nothing! Shit! There are no buts. You can't have this baby right now."

"You don't own me, Brian. You can't tell me what I can't do."

Brian slammed his hand down on the cushion again and shot up out of the sofa. "I don't give a shit if I own you or not, Carla. You can't have that fuckin' baby!"

"So what are you gonna do, Brian? Leave me if I do? You gonna be just like all of the niggas in the street and not take care of your responsibilities?"

Brian gritted his teeth again as a sharp pain throbbed behind his right eye.

Responsibilities.

A word the man who'd helped give him life had never known about. Brian swore he would never do what his sperm donor had done. He swore he'd never leave his children fatherless. Never leave them to fend for themselves. Never let them cry themselves to sleep at night wondering why their daddy didn't love them. Wondering what they'd done to make him disappear. He'd swore he'd never leave them alone to figure out what to do with the opposite sex. He swore he'd never force them to figure out how to be a man on their own.

Responsibilities.

He didn't want them. Didn't need them.

He wasn't ready.

He shook his head. "I gotta go," he said, grabbing his book bag and slinging it over his shoulder. Without saying another word, he rushed past Carla and ran outside.

As the door closed behind him, Carla called out his name. He paused for a moment. He was wrong and he knew it. Carla needed him. But he couldn't deal with this right now.

He walked off down the block, his destination unknown.

15

Deahnna stopped just outside of Jawan's classroom, took a breath, and held it for a few seconds before letting it out very slowly. Her hands were shaking a little, her palms slick with perspiration. Her skin was warm, despite having just been out in the crisp and biting October wind. She was schoolgirl nervous. Middle. Maybe high school. Nervous, excited, and fearful all at the same time.

She was about to go out on a date. Something she hadn't done in such a long time. For so long she'd closed herself off from happiness, which, in her experiences, had led to only pain, to heartache. She hadn't wanted to feel the hurt ever again, so her life became about doing what it took to survive, and about her son. It wasn't ideal and it was lonely at times, but at least she'd avoided even the possibility of being hurt again.

Yet there she was, seconds away from walking into a classroom to meet her son's teacher for a date. A date that, if she wasn't careful, could turn out to be much more.

That frightened and aroused her.

Of all the men in the city. Of all the men who'd ever tried to approach her with cocky and sometimes pitiful lines, and wry smiles, why had it been Jawan White who'd broken the invisible and practically impenetrable steel wall she'd had up? What had it been about him? His sexy smile? His deep-set brown eyes that seemed to be in deep thought? His personality that was inviting and comforting? His lean body that made her wonder how it looked without clothing?

Deahnna took another breath as her heart thumped with nervous anticipation beneath her chest. Of all the men who'd tried and failed, she'd never felt an instant connection with any of them. An almost kismet sort of sensation. Regina had said to keep her mouth shut about the stripping that she did. To let things develop. That when the time was right, she could then reveal the truth, if she needed to at all. Deahnna knew that Regina was right. Telling him too early was risky. It was better to keep that information buried. Better to let him get to really know her. To know what she was all about. When and if the time came, he would know that taking her clothes off in front of complete strangers didn't define her.

Hold the truth.

Lie.

The right thing to do, but so completely not what she wanted to do.

She didn't want to lie. She didn't want to pretend to be something or someone she wasn't. Yet as she inhaled, exhaled, and stepped into the room, she knew that if the moment came to talk about what she did part-time, her answers would be fiction disguised as truth.

"Hello, Jawan?" she said with a smile.

Jawan, who was sitting behind his desk, flipping through a textbook, looked up. He returned her smile and said, "Hey."

Deahnna looked at her watch. It was a quarter to seven. "I know I'm a little early. I just wanted to get out before Brian came home. I'll sit in the back while you finish with what you're doing."

Jawan shook his head. "You're fine," he said, closing his book. "I was really just passing the time."

"Are you sure? Because I don't mind waiting at all."

Jawan stood up. "Trust me. I'm sure."

Deahnna smiled. "OK."

Jawan said, "You look great."

Deahnna felt her cheeks grow warm, and was glad she had skin the color of burnt sepia. "Thank you," she said. She had on a pair of stretch blue jeans, and a beige slouch-neck sweater that hugged her waistline. Black leather calf-high boots were on her feet. It was a casual outfit, yet she knew the way it fit her was appealing to the eye. "You do too," she said.

Jawan grinned. He had on a pair of light blue jeans, a black button-down dress shirt, and black Skechers on his feet. "Best I could do on a teacher's salary," he said.

Deahnna nodded. "Well it works."

Jawan stared at her as silence claimed the room momentarily. His gaze was intense.

Deahnna stared back at him, her gaze just as deep.

Sexual energy crackled around them.

After a few seconds, Jawan cleared his throat. "So, are you ready to go?"

Deahnna said, "I am if you are."

Jawan grabbed his leather coat from behind his chair. "How do you feel about cartoons?" he asked, coming from behind the desk.

Deahnna looked at him with a curious eye. "Cartoons? I like the occasional *Tom and Jerry* and *Scooby-Doo!* if that's what you mean."

Jawan laughed. "Not quite. Have you seen the preview for the movie *The Last Airbender*?"

Deahnna thought about it for a moment, then shook her head and said, "No."

"Well, it's a new movie that's out. It's based on an animation series on Nickelodeon called *Avatar: The Last Airbender*. It's a great series with a great cast of characters. It's won a lot of awards."

"Really? I've never heard of it before."

"I have the whole series on Blu-ray. We'll have to watch it someday. You'll be hooked after the first episode. The movie that's out is the adaptation of the series, only with real people. Hopefully it will live up to the cartoon."

"And that's what we're going to see?"

"Yup."

Deahnna "hmm'd."

"You did tell me to pick the movie," Jawan reminded her.

She nodded. "Yes, I did."

"Would you rather I choose something else?"

Deahnna shook her head. "No. I told you to pick and you did."

"Yes, I did."

Deahnna smiled. "Before we go, I have to ask, is Grady still alive?"

"And kicking," Jawan answered.

Deahnna gave him a skeptical glare. "Hmm. I'll believe it when I see it."

Jawan shrugged. "That can be arranged."

Deahnna felt her skin grow warm again as Jawan watched her with a sexy gaze. She cleared her throat. "Lead the way, Mr. White."

They took a taxi cab to King's Plaza and caught the eight-thirty showing of the movie. They sat in the middle toward the top, where couples usually sat when they wanted or had been dared to do more than watch a movie. They shared a large popcorn, some Twizzlers, and had their own medium Cokes. Jawan leaned to his left. Deahnna to her right. They sat shoulder to shoulder for the entire film, which was an engrossing mixture of action, suspense, and comedy.

"So," Deahnna asked as they walked out, once the film's credits began to roll. "Did it suffice or disappoint?"

They were walking side by side. With each step, their hands lightly touched. Based on his personality, Deahnna had no doubt that Jawan wouldn't be bold enough to grab hold of her hand, but she wished he would.

Jawan smiled. "Definitely sufficed," he said, the tone in his voice higher with excitement. "I mean, it wasn't as perfect as the series, but it was damn close. I'm already hyped to see the next one!"

Deahnna nodded. "I have to admit, I'm looking forward to the sequel too."

"There's going to be a third also."

"Really?"

"Yeah. This is only one of a trilogy. There are a lot of characters you still haven't met."

"Wow. Well I have to say, after seeing this, I really want to see the cartoon series."

They were outside now. Deahnna tightened the belt of her suede coat and put her hood, lined with faux fur, over her head.

Jawan zipped up his coat and flagged down a cab that was fast approaching. As it came, he turned to Deahnna and said, "Disc one is in my Blu-ray player if you want to see it now."

Deahnna looked at him as he watched her intently. Once again, despite the frigid air, she felt warm. "How convenient," she said playfully.

Jawan said, "I was watching it last night. Wanted a refresher before tonight. All we'll have to do is press play."

Deahnna "mm-hmm'd." "Nice try. I bet you invite many ladies over to watch the *Avatar*."

He gave her a sneaky smile. "Only after they've seen the movie with me."

"Mm-hmm. And how many times have you seen it?"

"This is the first time. But I have a few dates lined up for tomorrow."

"Mm-hmm."

Jawan shrugged as the cab came to a stop in front of them. He opened the door. "I'm just trying to expose as many people as I can to the Ang and the crew."

Deahnna laughed and got into the cab. "Oh you're slick," she said. "I may have to take Grady with me tonight. I really don't know if it's safe for him to be with you."

Jawan chuckled. "So, does that mean that you're taking me up on my offer?"

Deahnna looked at him as she sat back against the cab's surprisingly comfortable beige leather seat.

Was she accepting his offer?

There was a whispering in her left ear. Words of caution being spoken.

Slow down. Yes, it feels right. Yes, it feels real, feels natural. Like the cliché: the start of something wonderful. But it always starts this way. It's always bells, whistles, butterflies, and singing birds. It's always a fairy tale. But you know what happens next. You know that the evil witch bringing the black dragon and the poisoned apples always appears. Besides, you haven't talked. Really talked. You haven't had to lie yet. You haven't had to pretend to be better than what you are.

Slow down. Go home.

Deahnna heard the words well, but found it hard to focus, because while caution sounded off on the left, words of encouragement were being yelled in her right ear.

Go for it!

Stop thinking!

It's right. It's real. It's been too damned long. You

need this, girl. Your mind. Your body. Your soul needs this. Say yes, and stop letting the past block you from happiness. The past is what it is. Stop thinking about witches and dragons and rotten apples. Say yes, before someone else does.

Deahnna looked at Jawan. At his sexy eyes, his sexually mischievous smile. It had been so long since she'd felt this way. So long since she'd been this open, this at ease. It was scary, yet exciting at the same time.

Say it!

Say it!

Say . . . "Yes," she said, her heart thumping as she took a leap of faith. "I'll come over."

Jawan smiled at her and then gave the cab driver his address. On the way there, he took hold of her hand.

16

Brian lay in his bed and stared up at a strand of a cobweb hanging from his ceiling. He was alone, his mother at her second job, which was good because he needed the solitude.

It had been a rough two days since Carla had given him the news. Pretending that everything was right and normal in his world had been taxing. The anxiety and stress bubbling inside of him was volcanic. Keeping himself from exploding was damn near impossible, and had he not had the peace tonight, he was certain he would erupt.

Pregnant.

Carla.

With a fucking child.

His child.

Brian yelled out, yanked one of his pillows from beneath his head and threw it across his room, sending it flailing across his dressing table, knocking over bottles of cologne, shaving cream, and deodorant. If her mind didn't change, if she continued to say that an abortion wasn't an option, then he was going to be a father.

Brian cursed out again, yanked his remaining pillow and threw it, sending it crashing against his computer monitor, which teetered back and forth. He'd told his mom that the PC had been a giveaway from the school. That as new PCs came in, they gave the old ones to deserving students who needed them.

It had been a lie.

The PC, a Dell with a Pentium processor, had been bought with money that he, Tyrel, and Will had taken after holding up a Chinese takeout restaurant toward the end of Jamaica Avenue.

Brian cursed. Slammed his fist against his wall. Cursed again.

Money.

He would need that now more than ever with Carla carrying his seed.

Money for Pampers, wipes, food, bottles, clothes, shoes, more Pampers, more wipes, more food, more bottles, more clothes, more shoes.

Money.

For strollers, cribs and playpens, toys.

Money.

Fucking money.

Money that Tyrel swore they could pull in by ripping off Old Man Blackwell.

Brian cursed, hit the wall again, then sat up, swung his legs off the bed on to the floor, and pressed on his right eyeball, the pain from a migraine hovering behind it.

Carla was pregnant. She swore an abortion was out of the goddamned question.

Pregnant.

Shit.

What the hell did he know about being a father? He'd never had one. Never had an example or a friend with one who he could learn from and emulate. So how the hell could he be a fucking father?

He stood up and paced back and forth in his tiny room. He'd felt the storm coming, but he'd had no clue it was going to be this damn bad. He pressed on his eye again, then jabbed his middle finger and thumb into his temples.

This shit was unfair.

So fucking unfair.

About to yell out and hit his wall again, his cell phone chimed.

A text message.

Carla had been bombarding him with them since he'd walked away. She'd cursed him, begged him to return her calls, cursed him again, said that he wasn't shit, apologized, said she was wrong, that she was sorry, then said how much she hated him, then loved him. He hadn't returned any of her messages.

He went to his phone.

The pregnancy didn't change what he felt for Carla. He loved her. And he was hurting her for something that she hadn't caused on her own. He exhaled. He would reply this time, because he hated knowing that she was in pain and feeling abandoned.

He grabbed his phone and looked at it. But the text wasn't from Carla this time. This time it was from Will.

Yo, son, come on. I know how you feel, but we need the money and we can't do this shit without you, son.

Brian stared at the message.

Money.

They needed the money.

And now he needed the money more than ever because he had fucked up.

He took a breath, hit the reply button, and typed two words that he knew he would regret.

I'm in.

17

Jawan couldn't believe it.

Deahnna was there with him.

In his bed. Naked. Breathing softly, evenly, peacefully. Her head was on his chest. Her right arm wrapped across his waist. Her right leg lying over his left. His left arm lay across her upper torso, his fingers caressing her smooth skin as though it would fall to pieces if he touched it too hard. He breathed in the scent of her shampoo. Strawberries and melon. Just like the commercials promised.

He was dreaming. He had to be, because this was just too perfect.

He closed his eyes. Counted to ten, sure that when he opened them, she would be gone and Grady would be lying in her place. He hit ten and opened them. She was still there. Still naked, still sleeping from the passionate and unexpected bout of sex they'd had. Unforgettable sex. Sex that moved mountains.

Dreaming.

Jawan swore that it was all a dream. Insisted on it. Insisted that after the movie, Deahnna had taken a cab home alone to her home. He hadn't been sitting beside her, her hand in his, his index finger lightly going over her knuckles. They hadn't looked at one another with lingering gazes. They hadn't arrived at his house, gotten out of the cab, and walked hand in hand up four steps to his front door.

"I only live a few blocks away," she said, waiting as he opened the door. "Down on Grant."

Jawan opened the door and flipped on a light. "That is close," he said. "After you."

Deahnna walked in. He followed, and closed and locked the door behind him. They were standing in a foyer. A flight of stairs leading up was in front of them, and a closed door was to their immediate left. The door was at the beginning of a tiny hallway, which led down to another door on the right.

Deahnna smiled. "Nice. Bigger than I thought. You have two floors."

"Three, actually. There's a basement. I rent out the top to a man and his wife and two girls. The basement's unfinished, but my washer and dryer are down there."

Deahnna said, "My apartment would fit in here."

Jawan laughed.

"My granny had a washer in her kitchen in an apartment she used to have in Brooklyn by Flatbush Avenue," Deahnna said. "She used to hang dry her clothes. I wish I had an apartment like that. Going to the Laundromat is a killer on the pocketbooks. You're lucky."

Jawan nodded. "I am. This was a foreclosure unit. I lucked into it a few years ago." He turned to his left and unlocked the door. "Welcome to my humble abode." As he pushed the door open, Grady meowed and pranced out to his leg. "What's up, Grady-Grade," he said, bending down and petting his companion behind the ear.

Deahnna "aw'd." "The famous Grady," she said. She bent down and, instead of shying away, Grady went to her outstretched hand.

"Grady!" Jawan said. "I thought you were supposed to be my watch dog? How are you gonna go to her for love without even feeling her out first?"

Caressing Grady underneath his chin, Deahnna looked up at Jawan. "He knows a good thing when he sees it. He doesn't need to feel me out."

As she moved from beneath his chin to beneath his belly, Grady purred and meowed as if to say, "Exactly."

"Don't worry, Grady," Deahnna said, putting her mouth closer to the cat's ear. "I won't let him hurt you anymore."

Grady purred again as Deahnna stood up and smiled at Jawan.

Jawan lightly and playfully pushed his companion to the side with his toe. "You have to leave sometime," he said to Deahnna with a sexy smirk.

Deahnna stuck her tongue out at him. He couldn't help but wonder what it would be like to suck on it as they kissed. He smiled and then said, "Come on in. Luckily my maid cleaned up today."

Deahnna chuckled. "A maid on a teacher's salary. Hmm. Maybe I need to give you my resume." She walked past him into a small front room with a computer sitting on a metal desk, a small black leather sofa, and a shelf system in the corner.

Jawan closed the door. "Trust me, I pay my maid a minimal salary. Somewhere along the lines of free per hour."

Deahnna laughed.

Jawan did too. "So this, as you can see, is my study."

Deahnna nodded. "Nice. I like the dogs playing poker on the wall."

Jawan smiled. "I thought it was a good fit here."

Deahnna raised her eyebrows. "Mm-hmm."

Jawan moved past her and clicked on a light in the next room. "This would be the living room/movie theatre."

He led the way as she followed, with Grady at her heels.

"Do you have hardwood floors throughout?"

Jawan nodded. "Yeah. Except for the kitchen. I actually put the floor down myself."

"A teacher and a handyman. Hmm."

In his best Jimmy Walker voice, from the show *Good Times,* Jawan smoothed over the moustache of his goatee and said, "Well, you know, what can I say?"

Deahnna cracked up with laughter. "OK, J.J. I love hardwood flooring. It makes the place look bigger and it's a lot more sanitary than carpeting."

"Yeah, but it's a bitch to clean. I sweep at least two, sometimes three, times a day to pick up dust and Grady's hair."

"I thought you had a maid to do all of that."

"Oh, I meant that she sweeps two or three times a day."

"Mm-hmm. Well, you can definitely tell you live alone."

"Oh yeah?"

"Black leather furniture, black lacquer coffee table. Silver lamps, Muhammad Ali and Michael Jordan on the walls. This place is definitely lacking a woman's touch."

Jawan shrugged. "I'm already paying my maid nothing to clean. I can't pay her any more to decorate, too."

Deahnna smiled and shook her head. "OK, Scrooge."

"Bah humbug."

They both laughed while Grady hopped onto the arm of the sofa and stared at them.

After a few seconds, silence settled between them as they looked at one another. Jawan cleared his throat. "So, do you still want to watch the *Avatar?* Or does my pitiful bachelor pad have you wanting to hightail it into a cab home?"

Deahnna looked at Jawan, then at the living room, before settling back on him. "I'm definitely ready for the show," she said.

"I was hoping you'd say that."

***

Jawan continued to caress Deahnna's arm as she continued to sleep peacefully. *That conversation didn't happen,* he thought, inhaling the fragrance from her shampoo.

No way.

This was definitely a dream.

They didn't sit on the couch, first side by side, watching the *Avatar* series on his big screen, before cuddling arm in arm. A dream. That's all it was. He hadn't really moved his arm and placed it around her shoulders. She hadn't really slid down and laid her head on his shoulder. His fingers hadn't caressed her arm, worked their way up to her neck, and then moved from her neck to her cheek. She hadn't moaned, hadn't turned her head, bringing her lips upward toward his. And somewhere during Ang's quest to save the world, they hadn't really begun to kiss softly, passionately.

Their tongues hadn't really danced slowly as his hands slid beneath her sweater and felt the smoothness of her belly, before working their way upward to her full, soft breasts. She hadn't moaned as he ran his fingers over her thick, erect nipples. She hadn't moaned louder as he eased the sweater off of her, unclasped her bra, and then took her breasts in his mouth.

A dream.

That's what this was.

A passionate, intense, fulfilling dream filled with kissing, nibbling, stroking, sucking, tasting, pushing, pulling, twisting, turning, circling, flipping, sweating, moaning, groaning, begging, demanding, screaming, exploding, bucking.

Just a dream.

Jawan took a deep breath through his nostrils, drinking in the figment of his imagination wrapped in his arms.

So sweet.

So delicious.

So soft.

So damned real.

He again soaked in the object of his desires and wants, and then kissed her softly on the top of her head. Deahnna stirred a little and burrowed herself closer to him.

Jawan smiled, closed his eyes, and hoped they wouldn't open again, because if this was a dream, it was definitely a dream he didn't want to wake from.

18

"Yo, what up, kid."

Brian gave his boy, Will, five and a one-armed hug. "Sup," he said.

"I'm glad you changed your mind, kid."

Brian shrugged. "I couldn't leave my boys hangin'," he said. He thought about his pregnant girlfriend and wished the situation were different.

"So we're your niggas again, huh?"

Brian looked over Will's shoulders. Tyrel was sitting on the couch, an Xbox 360 controller in his hand. Tyrel stared at him, his eyes hard, his jaw harder.

Brian stared back, his muscles tensing up. "Y'all never stopped bein' my niggas," he said, meaning it.

Tyrel scowled, then said, "Yeah, a'ight," and went back to playing his game.

Brian looked back to Will, who frowned and shrugged. Brian raised the right corner of his mouth and shook his head. He walked past Will, cursing himself for being irresponsible and not using protection.

He walked into the living room and sat down in a chair off to Tyrel's right. Neither he nor Tyrel said a word. Will came in a few seconds later and sat down on the couch beside Tyrel, but he too didn't speak. The only sound in the room was of the *Need for Speed* racing game Tyrel was playing.

Brian sat forward in his chair, rested his elbows on his knees, remained that way for a few seconds, and then sat back again. He couldn't get comfortable. He didn't want to be there, but had no choice but to be. Again he cursed himself for his irresponsibility.

Engines revved, brakes squealed, cars crashed and exploded as the friends watched soundlessly for four minutes until Will stretched and said, "So, the three niggateers are back again."

Both Brian and Tyrel turned their heads in his direction.

"Niggateers, nigga?" Tyrel said with an eyebrow raised.

Brian shook his head. He couldn't help it; he began to laugh. "That was mad corny," he said, laughing harder.

Tyrel joined in the laughter. "Where the fuck you get that shit from?"

Will, who was cracking up with them, shrugged. "I just made that shit up, son."

"Corny," Brian said, tears leaking from the corners of his eyes.

"Yo, you an idiot, nigga," Tyrel said, wiping at the corners of his eyes.

All three friends heartily laughed tension away from the room.

Tyrel looked at Brian. "Where you get this nigga from?" he said, motioning his head over in Will's direction. Brian shook his head. "I stepped in a pile of him back in third grade. I haven't been able to get the motherfucka from under my shoe since then."

Tyrel laughed even harder and said, "I have the same fuckin' problem."

All three friends laughed for a few more seconds before winding down.

Tyrel looked over at Brian when they did. "So, sup, nigga. You sure you down? You sure you don't need more time to think about shit?"

Brian shook his head as Carla ran through his mind. "Nah, son. I'm good."

"You sure, nigga? We don't need you to be backin' out and shit."

"I said I'm good, son. I'm in. No backin' out."

Tyrel watched him with a skeptical eye for a long second before nodding. "A'ight then. Let's plan this shit."

19

Deahnna was still smiling.

Three days and just two phone conversations had passed since her evening with Jawan, and the smile that had spread across her face as she'd taken the cab home at two in the morning hadn't gone away. As a matter of fact, instead of shrinking, her smile had actually grown wider.

She'd made love to Jawan.

It had been an unplanned and a very spectacular event. One that Deahnna had absolutely no regret over. The fear and apprehension she'd felt initially quickly disappeared as she and Jawan sat on the couch together, as though they always sat on the couch together. The familiarity, the connection, couldn't be denied. Their being at the dance had been no coincidence. It had been deemed that the time had come for them to get together, and fighting that just didn't make any sense. So as they sat on the couch, his arm over her shoulder, Deahnna refused to go against the grain. She wouldn't fight the desire to touch and be touched. She wouldn't hesitate when the touching became kissing. She wouldn't press down on the brakes when the kissing led to undressing. And she wouldn't stop when the undressing led to sex that made her toes curl.

Deahnna smiled as she walked down Jamaica Avenue on her way home, the October wind having no effect on her. Her time with Jawan had been so simple, so free, and so perfect. There was nothing that could have made it any more amazing. Well, no, that wasn't true. The only thing that could have made their time together even more incredible was if she'd had the opportunity to wake the following morning in his arms. Getting up and leaving hadn't been something she'd wanted to do, but Brian was home, and even though he was her child, there was still a certain level of respect that she felt she owed him.

Speaking of which, hopefully he'd be home when she got there. She and Jawan had another Friday night date scheduled, and, although it would only be their second date, Deahnna knew that more would follow. It was time to have a talk with her son, something they hadn't been doing much of lately.

She smiled as wind whipped all around her. Friday couldn't come fast enough. She was looking forward to seeing Jawan and his intense, brown eyes again. She hurried across the street, and as she did, her cell phone rang. She dug in her purse, pulled it out, looked at the caller ID, and then connected the call. "Hey, girl," she said.

Her friend, Heather, said, "And why haven't you called me?"

Deahnna laughed. She'd known this was coming. "I'm sorry, girl. I had a busy weekend."

Heather sucked her teeth. "Apology not accepted. You go out on a date on Friday, and I had to call your ass for details? Nope. Apology not accepted at all."

Deahnna laughed again. "Please forgive me," she said as the J train rumbled by overhead.

Heather said, "We'll see. Forgiveness will be based upon the amount of juicy details I receive. And considering how deep in the dog house you are at the present moment, the details better be very, very juicy."

Deahnna shook her head. "You're crazy," she said.

"No. I'm getting married in six months. I'm just simply getting my living-vicariously-through-you skills perfected now, because things will be changing drastically for us very soon."

"Whatever, Heather. You guys have no kids. Your lives won't change that much."

"Yet," Heather said. "We don't have any yet. But we will in about three months."

Deahnna stopped walking, while people continued to rush by her, anxious to get out of the cold. "What? What do you mean you will in three months? Heather, are you pregnant?"

"Huh? Hell no, I'm not pregnant!"

"But you just said in three months you'll have a child."

"I was talking about a puppy!"

"A puppy?"

"Yes. Ivan's brother's rotty is pregnant. In about three months, we're going to get one from the litter."

"And how exactly is that like having a child?"

Heather sucked her teeth. "I don't know, but, shit, I've heard so many people say that a puppy is worse than a child."

Deahnna shook her head and started walking again. "You're stupid, Heather."

Heather laughed. "Anyway, will you tell me how the date went?"

Deahnna smiled. "The date was very nice."

"OK. So what did you do? You didn't really just go to the movies, did you?"

"Yes, we did just go to the movies."

"Boring."

"It was not boring. The movie was excellent. And after the movie, we went back to his place to watch a DVD that the film was based on."

"Are you serious? That's what you did?"

"Yes."

"Boring," Heather dragged out again.

"It was not!"

"Whatever. So at least tell me that there were some extracurricular activities going on while the movie played."

"Well . . ." Deahnna paused and thought about the soft, deep kisses that led to both she and Jawan being naked in his bed. He'd been considerate with the way he'd moved inside of her. She'd felt every inch of him, as he did what had been necessary to make her climax, powerfully. Sex wasn't unfamiliar to her, but passion like that had been.

"Well?" Heather asked.

"Well, we did share a glass or two of wine."

"OK, and after the wine?"

"After the wine, I went home," Deahnna answered, deciding to keep to herself the information about the night of passion.

"That's it?" Heather asked. "That's all you did? Watch a movie, and then have wine and watch a DVD?"

"Yup."

"Was the DVD a porno? At least say that it was."

Deahnna chuckled. "No, it wasn't a porno. It was a cartoon version of the movie. Well, actually, the movie is based on the cartoon."

"So you went to the movies and then watched cartoons?"

"Yes, and we had a great time."

She couldn't see her, but Deahnna could tell Heather was rolling her eyes as she said, "That's so lame."

"It wasn't lame at all," Deahnna countered. "It was nice and intimate."

"And there was no sex? No kissing? Nothing?"

"Well, we kissed a little."

"But you still went home?"

"Yes."

"Well, then, that means that the kissing must not have been all that."

"Actually, the kisses were perfect. And just so you know," Deahnna said, arriving in front of her apartment building. "I didn't get home until after two in the morning."

"Two in the morn—"

"I'll talk to you later, sweetie."

"Wait a minute—"

"Bye." Deahnna laughed as she ended the call, and she laughed harder when her cell rang seconds later. She shook her head and hit the ignore button, sending the call to her voice mail. She could have told her how the night had really been, but Deahnna wanted to keep that night to herself. Heather would make her pay during her next hair appointment, but that was OK, because she knew her friend loved her. Besides, Heather was more bark than anything.

Deahnna smiled and then went inside, walked the few steps to her door, slid her key into the lock, and opened the door. As she walked in, Brian's bedroom door slammed shut. Deahnna frowned, took off her coat and hat, and hung them on the coat rack. The warmth of her apartment was welcomed, but before she got too comfortable, she wanted to get talking with Brian over with. She wasn't sure how he'd take the news. Hopefully he'd see it as no big deal, but if he didn't . . . Well, there wasn't much he could do about it anyway. At least he would know and not be blindsided if word got out around the school or neighborhood.

She slipped out of her white, made-for-comfort Payless sneakers and approached his door. "Brian?" she said, knocking on it. "Do you have a second?"

From behind the door, Brian said, "I'm busy right now, Mom."

Deahnna frowned. Although he hadn't said anything, she knew something was bothering him, because for the past few days, he just hadn't been himself. She said,

"Busy or not, I need to talk to you, so I'm coming in." She turned the knob and pushed the door open.

As he'd said, Brian was busy on his bed, lying down, his hands intertwined behind his head, staring up at the ceiling.

"Really busy," she said, her hand on her hip.

Brian groaned, but didn't say anything.

Deahnna went to the foot of the bed and sat down. "Brian," she said, looking at her son, "are you OK? Are you going through anything that you want or need to talk about?"

Brian closed his eyes.

It was obvious to Deahnna that he had something heavy on his mind.

His eyes still closed, he shook his head. "I'm good, Mom," he said, the tone in his voice clearly contradicting his words.

Deahnna breathed out softly. She wanted to ask him again if something was wrong, but knew there was no point to it. Whatever he was dealing with, it was something that he just wasn't ready to talk about yet. She said, "OK. But, honey, if anything is bothering you, I hope you know that you can come to me to talk."

Brian nodded, but didn't respond.

Deahnna frowned. "So, how was school?"

"School was school," he said.

"Nothing exciting, huh?"

"Nope."

Deahnna cleared her throat and smoothed out the pants of her scrubs. "So, did you have class with your English teacher today?"

Brian opened his eyes, and dropped his chin to his chest as he raised his head to look at her. He closed his eyes a bit. "Yeah. Why?"

"Just wondered. So, do you like Mr. White? I mean, is he a good teacher?"

Brian pulled his hands from behind his head and propped himself up on his elbows. He looked at Deahnna, his eyes revealing that he knew why she was asking the questions she was asking. He said, "You like him, don't you?"

She looked at him, and after a slight moment of hesitation, said, "Yes."

"I figured so. I saw the way you were with him at the dance."

Deahnna smiled, her mind going back to that night momentarily. "Hope I didn't embarrass you."

Brian shook his head. "Nah. You were cool."

Deahnna chuckled. "Good to know."

"Mr. White likes you too," Brian said.

"How do you know?"

"I saw the way he was with you at the dance, too. Besides, I asked him if he was feeling you."

"You did?"

"Yeah. He said he wasn't, but I could tell by his eyes that he was lying."

Deahnna felt herself blush. "I . . . I need to tell you something. The other night, when I came home after two in the morning—"

"You were with Mr. White, right?"

She looked at her son. For so long she'd seen him as her little boy, her little prince, but looking at him at that moment, she marveled at just how much older he appeared. The edge of his jaw line was sharper, his eyes were darker, more intense. Ever since he was little he'd had a kind of an old-soul quality to him, but looking at him now, Deahnna couldn't help but think that he'd experienced more than he should have.

She nodded, her eyes on her son's, and said, "Yes."

Brian flexed his jaw, gave a slight nod, and then said, "You fuck him?"

Deahnna's eyes widened, both the question and the

words used shocking her. But the shock quickly dissipated as her eyes closed to slits. "First of all, Brian, that's none of your business."

"But that's my teacher—"

"I don't give a damn if he was the president of the United States! It's still none of your damn business. Second, since when do you think it's OK for you to use that language with me?"

"I—"

"I am your mother, Brian. Not one of your boys. You can use that language outside with them and anyone else all you want, but you better never talk that way to me again. Is that understood?"

Brian dropped his chin a notch as Deahnna glared at him with a look that could kill. He said, "Yes."

Deahnna shook her head. "I can't believe you would ask me a question like that. I know I taught you better than that."

Brian frowned. "I'm sorry," he said, his voice low.

Still fuming, Deahnna said, "Damn right you're sorry. You better remember your damn place!"

"OK."

"Unbelievable." Deahnna stood up and headed out of the room. Before walking out, she turned, looked at him, and said, "And for the record, young man, not that I owe you an answer, but no, I did not fuck him."

Question answered with a lie, she turned, walked out of the room, and slammed the door shut behind her. She went to her bedroom to change, shaking her head.

As she removed her pants, her cell phone rang from inside of her purse. She reached for it, certain that it was Heather calling for details again.

But it wasn't.

She groaned. It was the strip club's manager, Marvin. Deahnna thought about ignoring the call, but ignoring calls from Marvin sometimes led to termination, and with the outstanding bills, the rent, and the groceries she had to buy, she couldn't afford to let the job go. No matter how much she hated doing it, stripping made for a necessary amount of extra income.

She hit the talk button. "Hello?"

"Hey, Deahnna. I know you don't work on Wednesdays, but I need you."

"Marvin—"

"Just hear me out. I just got a call from a friend of mine. His boy is getting married and they want to have the bachelor party at the club in two weeks."

"Marvin—"

"Deahnna. These are high rollers and they're not afraid to dole out the cash. I know you need the money, so before you say no, just say yes. I promise it would be worth it."

Deahnna sighed. As much as she wanted to say no, Marvin was right. She wasn't in a position to say no.

Reluctantly, she said, "OK. I'll do it."

"Good. You, Regina with her old ass, and Rhonda will be on. I'm feeling generous, so I'll split the money sixty/forty instead of the usual seventy/thirty."

Deahnna frowned. "OK."

Marvin ended the call without saying good-bye.

Deahnna tossed her cell on the bed, sat down, and covered her face with her hand.

Money.

It was a crime the way it held her hostage.

20

"Fuckin' liar. Fuckin' bitch."

Brian slammed his fist against the wall and cursed his teacher again.

"Right to my goddamned face!"

He slammed his fist against the wall again and lay back on his bed. He hadn't intended on disrespecting his mother with his question. The words had really just slipped out. But shit, she was out past two in the morning with his lying-ass teacher. What the fuck was he supposed to think?

"Lyin' bitch!"

Whatever respect he had for his teacher had just been lost. All the nigga had to do was say yes. That he was feeling his mother. That they had a date planned. Brian wouldn't have liked it, but he would have had to respect him for being upfront about it. But instead of being a man, what did the nigga do?

"Lyin' motherfucka," Brian said through his teeth.

He sat up, swung his legs off of the bed, and slumped forward, resting his elbows on his knees. He shook his head. He hadn't seen his mom pissed like that in a long time, and for a split second, he thought she was going to flip out and smack him. He would have to apologize again, he knew, but after she'd calmed down enough to know that his apology was sincere.

As for his teacher . . .

He'd have words for him, too.

Brian let out a breath as a police car sped by, its

siren screaming from the streets below. Just a couple of weeks ago, life had seemed so simple. School, his boys and, for the most part, their harmless escapades, and his relationship with Carla. Two weeks. It had all been gravy. Now he could barely focus on his schoolwork—something that had always come easy to him. His friendship with his boys, particularly Tyrel, was there, but definitely not the same. And his drama-free relationship with Carla was now ultra-complicated.

He groaned.

He'd finally called and sent text messages to Carla, apologizing for the way he'd run out on her, but just as he'd taken the liberty to ignore her many attempts to reach him, she too wasn't giving him the time of day. He missed the hell out of her. Missed her smile, her laugh, her soft hands, her kiss. More importantly, he missed her company. Her presence always made any of his cloudy days clear and blue.

He reached for his cell phone on his night table, found her number, and hit the talk button. She wouldn't answer, but it didn't matter. He just wanted to leave another message, telling her again how sorry he was.

"Hello?"

Brian snapped his head back. "Carla?" he said, his voice filled with surprise. "Is that really you?"

Carla exhaled into the phone. "It's me," she said, her tone even.

Brian straightened his back. "I . . . I didn't expect you to answer. I'm glad you did."

"I got tired of ignoring your calls."

Brian smiled. "I've missed you," he said. "I'm really sorry for freaking out the way I did. That shit just caught me off guard, you know."

"Well, imagine how 'off guard' I was when I missed my period," Carla said, the pitch in her voice rising slightly.

Brian frowned. "I know. I really didn't mean to be like that. It's just . . ." He paused, brushed his hand through his hair, from the back to the front. "I mean, a baby, Carla. Damn."

"Yeah, damn," Carla repeated. "Well, luckily for you, you don't have to stick around. But me, I'm stuck."

"You don't have to be stuck though."

"Brian," she said in a don't-go-there-again tone.

He exhaled. "I know, I know."

"I told you I don't believe in doing that, so it's not an option. Anyway, like I said, you don't have to stick around."

Brian cradled his forehead in his hand, cleared his eyes, and ground his teeth together.

So different, he thought.

Two weeks ago, things had been so fucking different.

He took a slow, deep breath. Let it out slowly, and said, "I'm not trying to go anywhere, Carla. I . . . I love you."

On the other end, Carla began to cry softly.

Brian took another deep breath. He hated to hear her cry.

"I . . . I'm scared, Brian," Carla said, her voice a wavering whisper.

Brian breathed out. "I know. I am too."

"My mom is going to kill me."

He nodded. "Yeah. Mine too."

"She doesn't even know I'm having sex."

"I'm sure my mom knows, but she doesn't think I'm doing it unprotected."

"We really screwed up."

He nodded again and sucked in his lips. "Yeah, we did."

Carla sniffled. "What . . . what are we going to do? I mean, I want to finish high school and go to college," she said, her sobbing heavier.

Brian gnawed on his bottom lip. He wanted to finish school and go to college too. He said, "We'll figure something out."

"I . . . I wish you were here. I just want to lie in your arms."

Brian smiled. "I can come over after your mom falls asleep."

"Are you sure?"

"I'm sure. Just text me when she falls asleep."

"OK. I love you, Brian."

"I love you too."

Brian ended the call, set his phone on vibrate, and then put it down and lay back on his bed. He closed his eyes, not to sleep, but just to relax.

Two weeks ago.

His mom and his teacher.

His boys and Old Man Blackwell.

Carla and their baby.

Damn, how quickly it all changed.

21

Jawan was on cloud nine.

He thought he'd been there before, but he'd been wrong. Cloud eight. Maybe. Or, if he was really being truthful, his relationship with his ex, Kim, had really hovered somewhere around seven. Seven and a half on the best of days.

Kim.

She'd broken his heart. Chewed him up and spit him out. One night before he was going to pop the question.

He'd had everything planned out. Barry White on the iPod, food—restaurant prepared—on standby, expensive champagne that had been painful to buy, but, for the occasion, worth it. He'd purchased twelve of her favorite candles—ocean mist—to position strategically in the living room, the bedroom, the bathroom around the tub. Locations where he was sure they would cap what was undoubtedly going to be a yes, with bouts of passionate and uninhibited lovemaking.

He was ready. Had been for months. But he wanted to wait until the right moment. And there was no better moment than the night of their second anniversary.

But the night before . . .

He'd been away at what was supposed to have been a three-day, mandatory educational workshop. It was supposed to end on a Friday afternoon, but the instructor for the workshop became ill, so they cut everything short by one day, therefore Jawan arrived home early Thursday evening. Kim hadn't been expecting him until Friday night.

He could have called her to tell her about the change in plans, but he wanted to surprise her. The drive home would be about four hours, putting him in Brooklyn by ten P.M. At that time, Kim wouldn't be sleeping, but she would be watching TV, wearing the silk leopard-print robe with just a thong on underneath. She liked to sleep that way. No bra. No T-shirt. Just the thong.

Jawan had missed her, and, on the ride home, he thought of nothing else but getting rid of the robe and thong the minute he walked into her place using the key she'd given him. What hadn't been in his thoughts was the image of opening her front door and seeing her stark naked, riding her happily married boss—whom he'd met at her company's Christmas party just a few months before—in the reverse cowgirl position.

Things had been ugly.

Kim screamed, hopped off of her boss, quickly covering breasts he'd been anxious to devour, and called his name. Then asked what he was doing there.

Her boss, Rick—Rick, who was twenty years her senior—cursed with eyes wide open, grabbed a pillow, placed it over his crotch, put his palms up, and begged Jawan to let him explain.

Jawan, completely out of body and mind, reacted before thoughts even materialized. He rushed, pushed Kim out of his way as she tried to stop him, and leveled Rick with a right to his jaw, knocking him out cold.

Jawan could have been in some serious trouble that night. But Rick had far more to worry about than pressing charges. His tail between his legs, and fearing a beating from his wife far worse than the one Jawan had given him, Rick never pressed charges.

Jawan, his heart shattered, simply got into his car and drove away. That night the food order was cancelled, the champagne bottle was smashed, and Barry White became Linkin Park. The next day, the ring was taken back to the store. After the millionth call, Kim finally got the message that he had no intention of speaking to her ever again.

Looking back on it, he really should have thanked Kim. She'd saved him from making the biggest mistake in his life. But he hadn't seen it that way at the time. For a long while, Jawan swore off of relationships. When the urge came, and it did because he was a man, he sought out cheap one-night stands. No feelings, no attachments. Just fucking to relieve the need. To hell with ever placing his heart in a woman's hand again. For two years he lived that way.

And then he chaperoned the dance.

And now he was on cloud nine. Hell—soaring above it.

He smiled and closed his briefcase. Enough grading papers. It was time to get home. Grady needed to be fed. He needed to eat. And then he needed to hear Deahnna's sweet voice—something he found he was needing more and more.

Deahnna Moore.

He shook his head.

She had to be a sorceress, because that was the only way to explain how the hell she'd shattered the wall he'd put up after Kim.

He smiled, stood up, and reached for his coat when his cell phone rang. He looked at it, wondering if Deahnna had beaten him to the punch. Hoping, actually.

But she hadn't.

He answered. "Nick the Dick with the ball and chain!"

His cousin laughed. "Not yet, dude. Not yet."

"Practically."

"But not yet," his cousin insisted.

Jawan laughed. "So what's up, man. You didn't call to tell me that you backed out, did you?"

"Nah, dude. No backing out. I'm all in swinging from the vines, just like I did in *Zartan: King of the Vagina Jungle.*"

Jawan cracked up. "That's a horrible title."

"Yeah, but the DVD sold out the wazoo. And I won an award for best performance of the year."

Jawan shook his head and laughed.

"Anyway," Nick continued. "I'm about to go and wrap up this shoot with twins."

"Of course," Jawan cut in.

"Yeah, of course. You know Nick the Dick is in high demand. Anyway, I wanna let you know that the bachelor party has been moved up. We're gonna be out there in two weeks. It'll be on a Wednesday night, so you're gonna need to get a sub for you for the next day, because we ain't leaving the party 'til six in the mornin'," he sang like Snoop Doggy Dogg.

"A Wednesday?" Jawan asked.

"Yeah, dude. My man, Doug, has a friend who owns a strip club in the city. We had to do it for that night because I won't have any free nights until my wedding night. I gotta go away for a couple of weeks to film in a special location. Puerto Rico, baby!"

Jawan nodded. "Nice."

"I'm about to be daddy damn Yankee up in that bitch!"

Jawan laughed. He morally couldn't do what his cousin did, but he did envy the lifestyle just a little.

"So anyway, dude, the details should be in your e-mail by now. I just wanted to call and make sure you get that sub lined up early."

"OK. Will do."

"Cool. Oh, how's it going with the teacher? You still seeing her?"

"She's not a teacher. She's my student's mother. And, yeah, things are still good."

"Cool. Well, a'ight, dude, I'm out."

"OK, man. See you in a couple of weeks."

"Definitely."

Nick ended the call and ran off to do his hours of hard labor, while Jawan slipped his cell into his pants pocket. "A Wednesday," he said. There'd once been a time when Wednesday had been the first of six days in a row of partying for him. But those days were long behind him.

He shrugged one shoulder. It wouldn't be the first of six, but he had a feeling he might need at least six days to recover. He laughed and slipped into his coat. Wednesday was two weeks away. Right now, he had a cat to feed and a cloud to continue floating on.

22

"So, Mr. White, I have to ask: were you born with your powers, or did you acquire them as you grew older?" Deahnna chuckled at her own question.

Jawan caressed her shoulder with his index finger. "My powers?"

Deahnna burrowed her head into his chest more and played with the hair just below his belly button, but above his crotch. "Yes, powers," she said.

"What do you mean?"

She smiled. "You're a sorcerer," she said.

That was the only way she could explain how she was in his arms, in his bed, instead of being at the place she despised. A place that she desperately needed to get away from, but couldn't find a way to replace just yet.

Marvin had been pissed that she'd called out on another Friday. She wasn't the best dancer he had, but she was good and did have a following. Marvin was losing out on some good money, and for that matter, so was she. But as much as she needed the money, she loved Jawan's company more, and so, money be damned, she hadn't hesitated to say yes when Jawan asked her out for another Friday night movie.

"A sorcerer, huh?"

"Yes. *Merlin*. I'm supposed to be at work right now, making sure I continue to have a roof over my head, and instead I'm here with you doing things I should be ashamed of."

Jawan trailed his finger down her arm and then over the nipple of her breast. "Should be?"

"Yes."

"But you're not."

"Only because of the spell you put me under."

Jawan laughed. "Well, I hate to break it to you, but I'm no Merlin. As a matter of fact, if anyone here is guilty of magic spells, it's you."

"Me?"

"Yes, *Desdemona*. Definitely you."

"And why do you say that?"

"Because since the night of the dance, I haven't been able to stop thinking about you."

Deahnna raised her head, and looked up at him as he looked down at her. *Those eyes*, she thought. *I could never get tired of gazing at them*. "You're smooth, Mr. White. Very smooth."

Jawan flashed a sexy grin. "If anyone here is smooth, sexy lady, it's you. Now, 'fess up. How did you slip your magic potion into my water at that dance?"

Deahnna laughed and batted her eyelashes. "A sorceress never reveals her secret."

"See?" Jawan said, tapping her playfully on her rear end. "I knew you were a master in the art of witchcraft."

Deahnna laughed and kissed his chest. "You're insane."

"I have to agree," Jawan replied with a nod. "I have been certifiable ever since you came into my world."

Deahnna's smile widened as she felt her heart flutter. It had only been a matter of a few weeks—a month—and yet she felt as though she didn't know life before Jawan.

Like the stealthiest thief in the night, he'd come in and stolen her most prized possession—her heart. And there was nothing she could do to stop him.

"Thank you for calling out tonight," Jawan said. "Your coworkers haven't been too mad, have they? I imagine not having that extra person puts them behind a little."

Deahnna was thankful that he could only see the top of her head, so that he wouldn't see her frown. During a previous phone conversation, she'd had to do what Regina suggested she do. She'd had to lie. He wanted to know what she did for her part-time job. She'd told him that she cleaned office buildings in the city with two other people. She didn't like lying to him, but things were going too perfectly to do anything but. It wasn't something she was proud of, but it was necessary, because she knew men like Jawan only came around once in a lifetime. She hated doing it, but she lied, and swore to herself that she would find a way to leave Marvin and the club behind.

"No," she said, the pitch in her voice lowering a little. "They're actually OK. They're just happy to see that I finally have a life."

Jawan laughed. "Yeah, my cousin feels the same way."

"Here's to baggage," Deahnna said, kissing his chest again.

Jawan kissed her on the top of her head. "Yes. Absolutely. Oh, I've been meaning to ask: have you told Brian about us yet?"

Deahnna sighed. Things had been strained between her and her son ever since she'd nearly slapped the taste out of his mouth when he'd asked if she was sleeping with Jawan. He'd apologized sincerely since then, but things just hadn't been the same.

There was a distance between them that never existed before, and Deahnna wasn't sure if the distance was related to her relationship with his teacher, or if there were other things on his mind. She'd tried on a couple of different occasions to talk to him, but he just closed himself off, and wouldn't say anything more than he was cool. "Yes, he knows," she said.

"I figured as much, by the I'm-gonna-beat-your-ass stares he's been giving me the past few weeks."

"I'm sorry. I'll talk to him."

"No need to apologize and no need to say anything. I can handle the stares."

"Still, I'm sorry."

"Brian is very protective of you and he doesn't want to see you get hurt."

Deahnna smiled. "I know."

"If I were in his shoes, I'd probably do more than stare."

Deahnna laughed. "Is that right?"

"Oh absolutely. I would have probably been expelled by now."

Deahnna laughed.

"No kidding," Jawan insisted.

Deahnna laughed hard for a few more seconds and then said, "Let me ask you: other than the stares, how has he been in class?"

"Other than the mean-mugging, he's been OK. A little disconnected, I guess. He's been doing the work like he always does, but he hasn't been participating the same. Of course, with him knowing about us, I can see why."

"I don't know," she said. "Sometimes I just feel like he's going through something. I can't get him to open up to me anymore. This is where having a man in the house comes in handy. I think he'd open up to a man more than he would me."

Jawan kissed her head again. "I can try to talk to him if you want. See if there is anything besides his being overprotective of you."

Deahnna raised her head and smiled. "You're a pretty special man, you know that."

"I'm just doing what you've put me under a spell to do."

Deahnna looked at him. At his eyes. Jawan stared back, his gaze unblinking. "Thank you," she said softly.

Jawan nodded. "Anything for you," he said.

Deahnna brought her lips to his.

Anything for me, she thought, kissing and mounting him.

Anything for me.

God, it felt so good to hear that.

23

He was going to be a father.

Brian rubbed Carla's flat belly. His seed was inside, growing slowly. A boy or a girl. His son or daughter. A father.

Brian passed his hand from side to side. In a few weeks, her stomach would no longer be flat, and in a few months, he would feel movement beneath his palm. See it, too. And that scared the hell out of him, because the reality that he had no choice but to accept it would be tangible.

A father.

He had no idea about the concept of being one, but his ideas were based on things he'd seen on TV and in movies. He grew up fatherless, his boys and the majority of the kids he knew along his block had too, so he'd never had a model to go by. He never had anyone discuss with him the rules of fatherhood. Never had anyone explain what to do when . . .

He wasn't ready.

But, of course, that didn't matter now.

The trigger had been pulled. The race was on. And in about eight months, he would cross the finish line. But during the race, he would have to step out of his lane for a moment to do something he didn't want to do, but had to.

Old Man Blackwell.

In a few days, he, Tyrel, and Will—the three-man cartel—were going to rip him off. It was a day Brian was dreading. Old Man Blackwell had never had his doors disrespected. Not because he had trip wires, motion sensors, armored guards, or walked around with a loaded .22 on his hip, a shotgun at his side, a samurai sword strapped to his back, and a can of mace in his pocket. Truth be told, for all the money that he dealt with on a daily basis, Old Man Blackwell could barely spell the word "security," because it had just never been something he'd ever had to worry about.

Everyone knew and loved the old man, and he knew and loved everyone. He was grandfather and uncle to some. Counselor and teacher to others. If you had a problem, Old Man Blackwell had an ear to lend and advice to give. Sometimes he even had money out of his pocket to offer. For those reasons, the old man could literally walk out of his store, leaving his cash drawer open, and no one would even think to go into it.

Rich, who worked there seven days out of the week, was called the security guard, but really he was just a guy to whom the Old Man was giving a final chance at life. The only "policing" Rich really did was to make sure that he came to work when he was supposed to, and that he came drug free.

Brian had a lot of love for Blackwell, and it was breaking his heart that he was going to do what no one had ever dared. But he couldn't diss his boys, his brothers. As badly as he wanted to, he just couldn't. And worse still, with his seed growing, he was going to need the money they stood to take. Life was just so fucking unfair.

"What are you thinking about?"

Brian opened his eyes and looked into Carla's almond-shaped brown eyes. They were lying in her bed, their foreheads inches apart. It was three in the morning. Brian had snuck over and snuck into her room after her mother had fallen asleep. He'd been doing that a lot more since Carla had dropped the bomb on him. He looked at her and forced a smile. "Just thinking about you," he whispered.

"Just me?"

"And the baby, of course."

Carla nodded. "I'm thinking about that too. Haven't really been able to think about anything else."

"Yeah. I feel you."

"We need to tell our mothers."

Brian frowned. His mother was going to be damn disappointed in him. He said, "Yeah. I know."

"When?"

He shrugged. "I don't know yet."

Carla took a breath and exhaled. "I've been thinking about how to do it, but I . . . I just don't know how."

Brian lifted a shoulder again. "There's really only one way to," he said. "Straight and to the point. It is what it is. We're having a baby."

Carla gave a half smile. "I guess."

Silence passed between them for a minute or two, before Carla took another breath and said, "Brian, can I ask you something?"

His eyes closed, Brian said, "Yeah?"

"Are you excited?"

"Huh?"

"About the baby."

Brian tightened his jaw. Was he excited about the baby? He looked at Carla as she stared at him, waiting for his reply. A few weeks ago, he'd seen nothing but fear and regret in her eyes, but looking at her now, he saw something else. Something that hadn't been there before.

Was he excited about the baby the way her eyes revealed that she was?

He wanted to say "Hell no," he wasn't excited. He wanted to insist—no, demand—that she get an abortion. But he'd hurt her once when he ran out and ignored her calls, and as much as he wanted to, telling her the truth was just something he couldn't do. She was in the same cold, black seawater as he was, but whereas he had nothing, he was the buoy she clung to.

He breathed out slowly. He would lie to save her, while the waters took him down another inch because it was what he had to do. He said, "Yeah. I am."

Carla smiled. "I am too," she said. She put her hand over his on her stomach. "The more I think about it, the more excited I get."

Brian did all he could to not frown. "Yeah."

"I've been thinking about names."

"You have?"

"Yeah. I like Israel for a boy and Indigo for a girl."

Brian nodded and raised his eyebrows. She'd spent some time on them. "Nice. Those are nice."

"Do you have any other names in mind?"

He shook his head. "No. But I like those. They should be the names."

Carla smiled. "I still can't believe I'm pregnant," she said.

Brian ran his tongue over the front of his top teeth. He couldn't believe it either. But he didn't say that. Instead, he said, "I need to get home before my mom gets up."

Carla frowned. "Oh, OK."

Brian rose from the bed and slid on his sweat pants and sweatshirt, and then put his Timberland boots on. When he was done, he looked down at Carla. She was looking up at him with sad eyes. Eyes that were begging him to stay just a little while longer.

"I'll hit you up tomorrow," he said, bending down and giving her a quick kiss on her lips.

"OK," Carla said, her voice softer than before.

Brian turned, headed to the door, opened it slowly,

and took a cautious glance toward her mother's bedroom door. It was still closed, and, from behind it, he could hear her mother's snoring. Without saying another word to her, Brian hurried on tiptoes past her mother's door, and left the apartment as quietly as he'd come in.

On his way out he'd heard Carla crying softly from her room. Her tears had made his steps lighter and quicker.

24

This has to be my last night, Deahnna thought. *Because I can't do this anymore. I just can't.*

She applied eyeliner around her eyes, then grabbed her blush to apply to her cheeks. Tears sat just out of sight behind her pupils. She looked at herself in the mirror before her. "Some cleaning lady," she said to herself.

She exhaled as hooting and hollering exploded from the main area of the club. Rhonda, one of the youngest girls in Marvin's "stable" was on the stage. She was the first to go on and perform for the private bachelor party going on. Rhonda, barely twenty-one, was a natural blonde with perky B-cups and a slender figure untouched by the pains and strains of childbirth. She was performing first. Regina would go next, and then it would be Deahnna's turn. After their solo performances, the three would perform together, making sure to send the groom-to-be off with a ménage à trois that was sure to get a standing ovation and make dollars fly.

Deahnna couldn't wait to get the night over with. She wanted to do the job, collect her money, and then rush out of there and never go back.

"I should do that," she said.

"Should do what?"

Deahnna turned. Regina had just come from the lounge area.

Deahnna shook her head. "Nothing," she said. "I was just thinking out loud."

Regina said, "Oh," and then went to her locker. She rotated a Master Lock on it, right, left, right, then removed it, opened her locker, and reached inside and removed a stick of deodorant. "It is crazy out there," she said, putting layers on under her arms. "Those guys are something. A couple of them are porn stars, or so they say, so don't be shocked when they proposition you. Of course, they don't have to be porn stars to do that."

Great, Deahna thought. She took a glance at the clock and willed it ahead four hours. Unfortunately, she hadn't been born with any mutant powers.

"Honey, you don't go on for another twenty minutes. Why are you not out there getting some extra cash just mingling? These men have money to spare. I'm telling you."

Deahnna frowned. Money. That was the reason she was there. The reason she'd given in to Marvin over the phone, and then again when she tried to back out earlier in the week.

Money.

That she needed.

That made her a hostage to the lack of respect she commanded.

Regina said, "Honey, I know you don't want to be here, but you are here. It may not be the ideal situation, but make the most of it and go get what these men are anxious to give up."

Deahnna frowned. "I know. I . . . I just hate this so much, Regina. I feel so . . . dirty."

Regina gave her an "excuse me" look, with her eyebrows raised and lips pressed firmly together.

Deahnna said quickly, "No offense."

Regina said, "Honey, you have a child you are doing all you can to provide a home for. There is absolutely nothing dirty about what you're doing."

Deahnna sat still for a moment, taking in Regina's comment. She hated her job, hated having to endure the shame she felt, the long, hot showers in the wee hours of the morning, just trying to wash off the filth she felt on her skin. But as she sat, unmoving, she had to accept that Regina was right. For her son, for her angel, she would do whatever she had to do. Filth be damned.

She looked at Regina and gave her a half smile. "Thank you," she said.

Regina closed her locker. "Your son is the one who needs to thank you, honey. Hopefully one day he will by being nice and successful."

Deahnna raised her eyebrows. "Hopefully."

Regina smiled. "Now, go and mingle and get some money."

Deahnna nodded. "OK."

Regina turned and hurried back to the private party. Deahnna looked at herself in the mirror.

For my son, she thought, picking up her lip gloss. For her son.

"His ass better pay me back," she said.

She stood up, took a deep breath and a final look at herself, then exhaled and reluctantly went out to mingle before her performance.

25

Jawan's head felt like it was going to explode. His eyeballs felt as though they'd swollen to two times their normal size. His nose ran and refused to let up, while his throat hurt, closing up on him slowly.

Of all times.

He slumped down on his couch and pressed his eyeballs with his thumb and index finger. *Of all times,* he thought again. He had to get sick now. The night of his cousin's bachelor party.

He groaned, and moved his fingers from his eyes to his temples. Applying pressure upon pressure would accomplish nothing, but he squeezed anyway. Squeezed and did his best to believe that the harder he did, the lighter his head felt. "Of all the times . . ." he said.

He released a heavily frustrated breath of air, looked over to the time displayed on his HD cable box, and moaned. It was almost twelve-thirty. Ten minutes off, actually. Nick's bachelor party started at eleven. Well, the part before the party actually began at nine, but Jawan needed rest. A power nap really. Just an hour or two to let the NyQuil he'd taken earlier die down in his system. Sleeping for just over three hours had not been his intention.

He'd awoken to the sound of his cell phone ringing. Nick, asking where the hell he was. Had it been anyone else, he would have said that he was in bed with a possible case of the swine flu, and that he was going to stay in for the rest of the night, and possibly even the next day. But it wasn't anyone else. It was his cousin, who was more like a brother, and no matter how bad he was feeling, he had no choice but to say that he'd gotten tied up taking care of some things, and that he would meet up with them pronto.

Nick, already halfway to not remembering anything that would happen that night, commented on a stripper's ass, and then told Jawan to get his ass down there before the "real" show started.

Jawan said he would.

Now he was on his couch, cursing the NyQuil for doing nothing but leaving him feeling slightly off center.

He moaned and groaned again and then stood up. If he was going to go, then he just needed to go. Forget about the sinus pressure. Say to hell with his eyes feeling like they were popping out of their sockets. Just walk with a wad of tissues in the pockets, and go and let it all hang out, and pray that he wouldn't die until the next day.

"Of all the damn times," he said once more.

He grabbed his wool coat from the closet, slipped it on, zipped it up, and then, after patting his pocket to double-check that he had his wallet, he grabbed his cell phone from the computer desk, where he'd put it to charge as he'd showered and dressed.

He'd missed his good night call with Deahnna. For the past couple of weeks, before he shut his phone down and went to sleep at night, he called Deahnna to wish her a good night's sleep. He liked to go to dreamland with the sound of her voice being the last thing he'd heard. She must have been preoccupied too, he thought, taking a quick scroll through his call history, because she hadn't called either.

"Maybe she thinks the calls are corny," he said, slipping the phone into his pocket. "Maybe her no call is a nice, subtle hint."

He shrugged, promised himself to ask her the next time they were together just what she thought of the calls, grabbed his keys, and walked out the door.

Twenty minutes later, after hopping on the J train and then transferring to the A train to get into the city, he caught a cab and took that to the strip club.

The pressure in his head was still there, but the cold, biting October air helped to make his nose stop running . . . or the medicine had finally kicked in and done something positive. Either way, at least the only thing he'd have to deal with would be the throbbing in his head from the sinus buildup, and the loud, bass-heavy music coming from inside.

After convincing the bouncer at the entrance that he was there for his cousin's party, Jawan walked in and was greeted by the sight of an older female on the main stage wearing nothing but white cowboy boots, twirling around a silver pole with one leg wrapped around it, while her D-cups swung freely. The dancer clearly had one foot out the door on her way to retirement, but as Jawan stood still by the door, he couldn't deny, as she dropped down to her knees, bent over, and thrust her ass into the air as though to say that she loved getting it from behind, that she had skills.

Nick's eight-man entourage hooted, hollered, whistled, clapped, and tossed a bevy of dollar bills on to the stage as the older dancer finished her set.

Jawan shook his head and smiled. It had been a while since he'd been to the strip club. His headache diminishing, he looked past the round tables and black chairs, and spotted Nick, who was sitting with two other guys toward the front center of the stage, throwing down a shot and tossing his own dollar bills. Jawan laughed and was glad for the rest he'd gotten, because he had no doubt that the night was going to be long and crazy.

He made his way in the dimly lit club over to Nick. “What’s up, man,” he said, slamming a hand on Nick’s shoulder as he gave one of Nick’s boys a pound, and the other a nod.

Nick looked up at him through half-glazed eyes. “JawanaMan! It’s about fucking time, dude!”

Jawan nodded. “Yeah. My bad. I got busy.”

“That pussy must be real good for you to get that busy,” Nick said, laughing and looking at his boys.

Jawan laughed too and sat down. As he did, a topless waitress came over. Knowing that he shouldn’t drink with the medicine in his system, he ordered a Jack and Coke anyway. “So what’s up?” he said to Nick, who’d ordered a Hennessy and Coke. “Did I miss anything?”

Nick slapped his palm down on the tabletop. “Shit, dude, you missed enough.”

“Yeah, well, it’s probably good that I did anyway. You know I’m on a teacher’s salary.”

“Dude,” Nick said, leveling his eyes at him, “I keep telling you that you could have some serious cheese in your bank account.”

“Yeah, yeah,” Jawan said as the waitress brought their drinks over. “I’m just not as brave as you are.”

“Dude, it ain’t about being brave. It’s about fucking and getting paid.”

“Yeah, yeah. I hear you.”

“Yeah, yeah,” Nick mocked. “You’re not hearing shit. But you go ahead and struggle with your teacher’s salary. I’ll keep struggling with this.” He pulled out a thick wad of money rolled together. Jawan didn’t know how much was there, but the bill on the outside was a hundred dollar bill.

“Yeah, yeah,” Jawan said, downing some of his drink.

“Yeah, yeah,” Nick mocked again, to his boys’ delight. “Anyway, dude, you keep your teacher’s salary in your pocket. I got you.”

Jawan shook his head. "No way, man. You're the one who's getting married. You shouldn't even be spending any money."

Nick said, "Dude, it wouldn't be any fun if I wasn't."

Jawan thought about it for a moment and then nodded. "I feel you. That being said . . ." He reached into his pocket and pulled out his own stack of money. "It's not as thick as yours, but I'll be all right."

Nick laughed. "A'ight, cool."

"All right, all right, gents!" the DJ yelled from the booth. "Give another round of applause for Prairie Dawn!"

Jawan, Nick, and the rest of the guys cheered and clapped loudly.

"Now, we gave you the schoolgirl, and the experienced cowgirl. Get those ones, fives, tens, and twenties ready, because coming to the stage right now is the one, the only, Foxy Brown!"

Everyone turned their attention to the stage as the lights dimmed and the song "Pony," by Ginuwine, began to play.

Slowly, Foxy Brown emerged from the back, moving seductively to the song's entrancing rhythm, with her back to the eager crowd. She had on a black thong and a black sheer top. On her feet she wore a pair of four-inch black pumps.

She moved slowly, rhythmically, making her way out of the shadows into the light at the center of the stage. Nick and all of his boys were whistling, clapping, and calling out to Foxy Brown, telling her to turn around as they tossed money at her.

But Jawan . . .

Unlike his cousin and everyone else, he sat stone still with his drink in his hand and an inhaled breath trapped in his lungs.

He wasn't a rear end connoisseur, but as he sat staring at the dancer before him, he had the sick feeling that he knew that ass very, very well.

He stared.

As Foxy Brown worked her hips in a way he'd seen worked before.

At a dance.

He stared.

As the music thumped. As Nick and his crew cheered. As dollars flew. As Foxy Brown, her shoulder-length hair lying around her shoulders in an all-too-familiar manner, turned around slowly with one hand grabbing the pole behind her, while the other cupped her breast.

Jawan stared.

As the music died around him. As Nick and the other guys disappeared. As the lights suddenly beamed like sunlight shining bright in the middle of the day.

He stared.

As his heart raced a thousand times faster with each passing millisecond.

He stared and then released all of the air he'd been holding as Foxy Brown stared past him.

"What the fuck?"

He slammed his glass down, causing much of its contents to spill over, and rose from his chair.

"What the fuck?" he said again.

On the stage, Foxy Brown looked at him, screamed out, "Oh my God!" and covered herself.

Jawan shook his head and tried not to believe what he was seeing. Who he was seeing. But no matter how hard he shook, the sight of her would not change.

Deahnna.

In front of him.

Center stage.

He slammed his brows together as the music stopped. "You're . . . you're a stripper?"

Deahnna shook her head as tears erupted from her

eyes. "Jawan," she said, her voice trembling. "I . . . I . . . I can explain."

Jawan said again, "You're a fucking stripper?"

"J . . . Jawan, please!"

"Dude," Nick said, putting a hand around Jawan's arm.

Jawan roughly pulled his arm away and backed away from the table. "A stripper?" he said again. He shook his head as the pressure there and behind his eyes came back tenfold. "A stripper?"

He looked at Deahnna as she called his name again.

"A stripper? Fuck!"

He turned and, while both Deahnna and Nick called his name, stormed out of the club.

26

No! No! No!

Tears clouding her vision, Deahnna stumbled back into the dressing room, pressed her back against the wall, and sank down to the ground, drawing her knees up to her chest.

No! No!

She buried her head between her knees as her shoulders shook with each hard sob, as she relived the nightmare she'd just experienced minutes ago when she laid eyes on Jawan, who'd been staring at her with eyes filled with shock and disgust.

"No!" Deahnna said, her throat tight, her chest tighter. "No!"

She couldn't believe it. Tried not to. Tried to will herself to wake up from the very, very bad dream she was having. *Please*, she begged. *Please let me be dreaming. Please don't let this be real.*

She cried and felt her heart break and shatter into an infinite number of fragments as she watched behind her closed eyelids, in horrific high definition, a replay of Jawan shaking his head and then storming out of the club. Over and over and over in the span of a few minutes. "No," she said again.

"Honey?" Regina said, placing a hand on her shoulder. "Was that him?"

Her head still buried, Deahnna nodded.

"Oh, honey," Regina said, her voice filled with sympathy. "I'm so sorry."

Deahnna raised her head slightly and looked at Regina through her tears. "Why did this have to happen?"

Regina shook her head. "I don't know, honey."

Tears fell harder and faster as Deahnna buried her head again.

"What the fuck is going on?" the club's owner, Marvin, yelled, stepping into the room. "Deahnna, what the hell?"

Unable to speak, Deahnna kept quiet and kept her head buried.

"Marvin, just give her a break and leave us alone for a minute, all right?" Regina said.

"Give her a break? Are you kidding me? I have paying customers out there wanting to know what the hell's going on! I'm losing money here. I don't have a minute to give."

"Well, Marvin, you're just going to have to do that."

"But—"

"Marvin, I can take my dancing and my other services elsewhere."

"But, Regina, this is a bad look."

"Christ, Marvin! Leave us alone or tonight will be my last night."

Marvin groaned, cursed, and, seconds later, left the room.

"Pain in the ass," Regina said.

Deahnna continued to cry while Regina rubbed her back. *Why me?* she wondered. She sobbed and watched again as Jawan stared at her. The look in his eye . . . She would never forget his pained expression.

"Let me help you up," Regina said, grabbing her hand.

Deahnna didn't want to, but she stood up and put her head against Regina's shoulder as Regina led her over to her chair. "Have you tried to call him yet?" Regina asked as Deahnna sat down. She reached over, pulled a tissue from a box, and handed it to her.

Wiping her eyes, Deahnna shook her head.

Regina pursed her lips. "Where's your cell?"

Deahnna blew her nose. "There's no point in me calling," she said. "After that look on his face . . ." She paused and a flood of tears fell from her eyes again.

Regina grabbed a handful of tissues and handed them to her. "Just try to call him, honey."

Deahnna shook her head again. "I . . . I know he won't talk to me, Regina. He was so disgusted with me. I saw it in his eyes. He hates me."

"Honey, you don't know that."

Deahnna looked up at Regina while she wiped her nose. "You didn't see his eyes, Regina. Trust me, he hates me."

Regina gave her a look as if to say, "Come on, don't be so melodramatic. I'm sure he doesn't hate you, honey. He was just shocked as hell, that's all. But he doesn't hate you. Not after the things you've told me about him."

Deahnna blotted the corners of her eyes. "Why? Why did he have to be here?"

Regina raised her eyebrows as the corners of her mouth dipped. "It's a small world, honey. Even here in New York City."

Deahnna strangled the tissues in her hand. "I . . . I can't believe this happened."

"Call him, honey."

Deahnna shook her head. "I don't think he'll answer."

Regina frowned, went to her locker, opened it, and removed her cell phone. She went back to Deahnna. "What's his number, honey?"

"I don't want to get you in the middle of anything, Regina."

"You're not getting me in the middle of anything, honey. I'm just dialing the numbers. You're going to be doing the talking. I figure there's a better chance of him answering the call from a number he doesn't recognize than there would be if your number showed up on his ID."

Deahnna shrugged. "I don't know."

"Just give it a try, honey."

Deahnna frowned, wiped at her nose and eyes again, and, after a reluctant second, recited Jawan's cell phone number to her. Regina made the call, and then, after making sure it was going through, handed it to her. Deahnna took it and put it to her ear. As it rang, the image of Jawan staring at her, shaking his head, and leaving flashed in her mind again.

God, what he must think about me, she thought.

The phone rang once, twice, a third time, and then went to voice mail. She ended the call and extended the cell back to Regina. "I told you," she said, her voice filled with disappointed frustration.

"Call him again, honey," Regina said. "And this time, leave a message."

Deahnna sighed. "Regina . . ."

"Just call."

Deahnna frowned again and then redialed Jawan's number. This time the voice mail clicked on right away. She said, "Jawan, I'm so, so sorry. Please call me. Please. I want, no, I need to explain what you saw. It . . . it's not what you think. Please call. I . . .I love you."

She ended the call, and handed the phone back to Regina as tears fell from her eyes and ran down her cheeks.

Regina rubbed her back. "Go home, honey," she said softly. "Go home and get some rest."

Deahnna shook her head. "That's not going to be possible."

"Well, just try, OK?"

Deahnna wiped her eyes and nodded. "I can't believe he was here."

“Six degrees of separation, honey. We all know somebody who knows somebody.”

Deahnna frowned. “This is so unfair.”

“That’s life, honey. Now, go home. Give him some time, but he will call you back.”

“How do you know?”

“Because he left instead of confronting you.”

Deahnna shook her head. “I don’t know.”

“Just give it time, honey. OK?”

Deahnna looked up at Regina. “OK,” she said. “I’ll try.”

“Good. Now, before Marvin has a conniption, let me see if I can help salvage the night for his ass. Call me when you get home, OK? If I don’t answer, just leave a text.”

Deahnna gave her a half smile. “I will.”

Regina gave her a kiss on her forehead, and then turned and left, leaving Deahnna alone.

Deahnna sat still as tears leaked from her eyes slowly. She took a breath and let it out slowly. *Why me?* she wondered again.

Terrance.

Marc.

Now Jawan.

Three men. Three different levels of pain and unhappiness.

As her tears fell, she couldn’t help but wonder just what it was that she had done wrong in her life.

27

A stripper.

A goddamned stripper.

No way. No damn way.

Jawan took hard, slow, angry steps. Deahnna was a stripper. Had he not seen it with his own eyes, he would have never believed something like that was possible. Had he not watched her back out onto the stage wearing nothing but a barely there thong and a see-through top that was practically the mother of see-throughs, he would have never ever believed . . .

"Shit!"

He stopped walking, turned, and looked back toward the club, which was a half a block away. He stared at the purple neon sign. CLUB ECSTASY, it read. Ecstasy. A place where men or women went to escape the reality of everyday life and lose themselves for an hour, or two, or three or more as they stared at tits and ass that they could only long to have. Tits and ass that were paraded and gyrated in front of them, teasing them, causing them to be voluntarily robbed as dollar bills, which a large majority of them needed at home, disappeared from their hands. It was the perfect legal crime. And with his own eyes, Jawan had watched as Deahnna played the ultimate role as Bonnie without Clyde.

"Shit!" he said again. He shivered, though not from the sharp, nighttime wind. "Shit!"

His cell phone rang. He grabbed it from his pocket and looked at the ID. A number he didn't recognize appeared. He let it go to voice mail, and then turned his cell phone off. Without knowing who the caller had been, he was sure it had been Deahnna. He shook his head, cursed again, and then turned away from the club. Of all the things he thought he'd ever have to deal with, this hadn't been one. And to think he'd hopped out of bed, sick, for this. He shook his head again and headed for an idling cab at the corner.

"Yo! Jawan! Dude!"

Jawan didn't want to, but he stopped walking and turned to see his cousin, Nick, running up to him. *Damn,* he thought. What a way to send his cousin off. He frowned.

"Dude," Nick said, coming to a stop, huffing in front of him. "What the fuck just happened?"

Jawan gritted his teeth and said, "I don't know, man." He breathed out heavily through his nostrils. "I really don't fucking know."

"You know that chick from the stage?"

Jawan looked over his cousin's shoulder toward the club, and, with his eyes focused on the neon purple, nodded. Through his teeth he said, "Yeah, unfortunately I do."

"Who is she?"

Jawan flared his nostrils and sucked his lips in. "Do you remember the female I told you about?"

"The teacher?"

"My student's mother."

"Oh yeah."

"Well, I'm sorry I was rude and didn't introduce you two."

His eyes opening wide, Nick said, "Shit, dude. You serious?"

Jawan raised his eyebrows. "Wish I wasn't."

"Damn," Nick said. And then he broke out in laughter.

Jawan gave his cousin a hard glare. "There's nothing funny about this, Nick."

Nick continued to laugh as he shook his head apologetically and put a hand on Jawan's shoulder. "I'm sorry, dude, but this shit is hilarious."

Jawan pushed Nick's hand from his shoulder. "Fuck you, Nick."

His outburst only made Nick laugh harder. "Don't flip out on me, dude. I wasn't the one up on the stage about to get buck naked."

Jawan shook his head at his cousin's insensitivity, and fought to not throw a punch at his face, which he knew would have been very, very wrong. After all, Nick had done nothing wrong. But, damn, did he want to hit something.

"A'ight, a'ight," Nick said, wiping tears away from his eyes. "My bad, dude. I'm sorry, for real."

Jawan frowned, but didn't say anything.

"I guess you didn't know she moonlighted as a show-me-what-you-got kind of chick, huh?"

Jawan shook his head. "Nope."

"So what are you gonna do?"

"I have no idea, man. Shit. No fucking idea."

"Guess you're not coming back inside."

Jawan's frown dipped lower. "Nah, man. I'm sorry about fucking up your night."

"Shit, dude. My night's not fucked up. Your girl's not out there, but the other chicks are back out on the stage."

Jawan nodded. Deahnna hadn't gone back out. He couldn't decide if that pleased him or pissed him off more. He looked at his cousin. "I'm gonna go home, man."

"You sure you don't wanna come back in, dude? I'm willing to bet that some shots of Hennessy might do you some good right about now."

Jawan shook his head. Although drowning his sorrows sounded like just the remedy he needed, the thought of going back in there was just not one he could fathom. "I'm sure, man."

Nick shrugged. "I feel you, dude. This is a real fucked-up coincidence. I mean, shit, of all the clubs we had to come to."

Jawan gave a curt nod. "Yeah, of all the clubs," he said, looking at the neon sign again.

"You gonna talk to her?"

"I don't know, man. Right now, I just really don't know. I'm kinda just barely holding it together right now, you know?"

"Yeah. I can imagine."

No, you can't, Jawan thought, but didn't say. "Anyway, man," he said, putting his hand out. "Go back in and get fucked up. I'll catch you in a few weeks for the wedding."

Nick took his hand and the two embraced in a one-armed hug. "A'ight, dude. I hope shit works out for you."

Jawan stepped back. "Thanks."

"And if it doesn't, don't sweat it. I have some banging chicks I can introduce you to."

Jawan forced a smile. "All right. But don't count on them roping me in to the business."

Nick laughed. "They can be very persuasive, dude."

"Yeah, OK."

More laughter from Nick. "Cheddar, dude. The business is all about cheddar."

"Yeah, yeah. All right, man. Take it easy. Try to remember what you did tonight."

"Shit, if I do that, then the night will be a bust. Anyway, if your chick comes back out, I'll give her your regards."

Jawan shook his head. "Not funny, man. Not funny."

"Not for you, JawanaMan. But it's one hell of a story for the fellas."

"Man . . ."

"Hey, they're gonna want an explanation."

"Yeah, whatever, man. See you in a few weeks." Jawan frowned, then waved, turned, and headed for a different cab, sitting at the end of the block.

"A'ight, dude. Take it easy."

Jawan walked to the curb, checked with the cab driver to see if he was taking fares, then, after confirming that he was, Jawan hopped into the back, which smelled like stale cigarettes and pina colada, gave the driver his address, and slumped back against the seat.

As the cab pulled off and headed down the congested, pothole-laden road, Jawan shook his head. Deahnna was a stripper. He'd known his night was going to be crazy. He just hadn't expected this level of insanity.

He closed his eyes, and as strange as his night was, a random thought ran through his mind.

Why the hell were cab rides always so damn comfortable?

28

Two days later, Brian sat in his English class sweating, although it wasn't from the heat in the room, of which there was none, since the school's boiler had broken down earlier in the day. Brian sweated from the anxiety coursing through his veins. From the nervous tension that had his muscles stiff. From the weight bearing down on his shoulders, making it difficult for him to breathe.

In a few hours he, Tyrel, and Will were going to pay a visit to Old Man Blackwell. At eleven-thirty, to be specific. That's when Blackwell closed up. That's when he would be counting all of the money he'd brought in from everyone's payday.

It was all planned out in three easy steps.

Step one: they would roll in before the doors were locked. Step two: they'd take out Blackwell's faux security guard, Rich, and then instruct the old man to give them all of the money he had. Step three: they'd pocket all of the cash and then quickly make their getaway.

One. Two. Three.

Simple.

They'd be dressed in their usual black attire, with black ski masks and black gloves. Just as he'd insisted the last time, Tyrel would be bringing the .45s, not to use, but just to have as an extra motivator in case Blackwell considered putting up even the least bit of resistance. Planned out, and if executed properly, they'd be done and back at Will's playing the Xbox 360 before midnight.

Brian gnawed on his bottom lip and wiped sweat from his forehead. Every fiber of his being was telling him not to go through with it. That something was going to go wrong. That the plan was just too perfect.

He wiped sweat away from his forehead again and looked over at the substitute teacher sitting where Mr. White usually sat. The word was that Mr. White had come down with the flu. This was the second day in a row now that he was out.

Brian was glad that he was. Ever since finding out about his relationship with his mother, Brian had been like a strand of fishing wire being pulled in opposite directions. He was taut, ready to snap. His animosity for his teacher, combined with the stressful situation with Carla, and the pressure from his boys to do what he didn't want to do, Brian didn't think he could hold back from exploding on his teacher—something he'd been struggling against doing. Mr. White was dating his mom. He'd lied about it to his face. Whatever respect he had for the man was now gone.

He took a breath and let it out slowly as he looked up at the clock. The day would be over in five minutes. He'd head over to Carla's for a couple of hours and somehow pretend that nothing was bothering him, and that he was just as excited about the baby as she had become.

Somehow.

Then he'd head over to Will's to get the dirty deed done. All for money that he needed.

Brian took another full breath and blew it out hard and fast. A cloud was hovering over him, thunder rumbling and growing louder. In a few hours that thunder would become deafening. He only hoped that lightning wouldn't flash and strike him down. But somehow he didn't think that he could escape the inevitable.

29

Deahnna was crying. It felt as though she'd been crying nonstop since Jawan stared at her with wide, stunned eyes.

Jawan.

God, she missed him. It had only been two days, but those two days felt like an eternity. She'd tried calling him, both on his cell and at home, but just as had been the case the night of his discovery, she'd gotten nothing but his answering machine at home, and a message stating that his voice mail box was full on his cell.

She sobbed hard and squeezed her eyes shut tightly. She just wanted the tears to stop. She wanted the image of Jawan looking at her with disappointed disgust to leave her alone. But, unfortunately, squeezing them only made the tears fall harder, and the image clearer.

But she deserved that, didn't she?

For her unsavory part-time profession. For lying when she'd had the opportunity to tell the truth.

She deserved the heartbreak she was now enduring.

She turned onto her side and burrowed her head into her pillow. Thankfully, Brian hadn't come home. She'd managed to hold herself together when he was around, but tonight she knew that wasn't going to be possible. She needed to be free. Needed to break down. Needed to let the tears of guilt, shame, and regret fall freely.

Guilt for her lies.

Shame for showing men what she concealed beneath her clothing.

Regret for not being strong enough to go with her gut and just skip the bachelor party altogether.

Deahnna cried and hoped Brian wouldn't be home for a few hours. She had a well full of tears to get rid of.

30

"Jawan, I . . . I'm sorry about lying to you. I just didn't know how to tell you the truth. Please believe me, I don't enjoy stripping. It's degrading, it's shameful. It breaks me down every time I do it. But, and as much as I hate admitting this, it's just been . . . necessary for me. I make just enough at the hospital to stay afloat. I've tried finding another full-time administrative position that pays more, but those jobs have been hard to come by, so obviously the next alternative was to find a part-time job. Stripping—God, I hate even saying that word—but stripping was never in my plans, but with the rent, the bills, food, and clothes to buy, taking my clothes off has been the only part-time job that's paid me the supplemental income Brian and I need. It's also been the only thing flexible enough with the hours that I could find.

"Please, Jawan, please. I hate doing it, but I have Brian to take care of, and I would do anything, *anything,* for my son. You don't have a child, so you couldn't possibly understand how it feels to be willing to sacrifice your soul for your child. And please believe, Jawan, that I have done that. I sacrifice a part of me every time I remove my clothing for dollar bills.

"Jawan, I care so much about you. I agonized with deciding whether to lie or to tell you the truth. It is truly one of the hardest decisions I've ever had to make. The day I lied to you . . . God, I wanted to be honest, and for a second I almost was. But I was scared. Scared of losing you. You've been the best thing that's happened to me in a long time. Since Brian's birth, really. The way you make me feel . . . Jawan, I don't want to lose you. You make me feel so alive, so special. You make me feel like I'm worth something. Please give me a chance to explain. I love you. Call me, OK?"

Jawan hit the stop button on his answering machine. This was the first of Deahnna's messages that he'd actually listened to. For two days he'd avoided hearing her. He didn't want to listen to her explanation. He didn't want to hear the sweet sound of her voice, because that would break down the wall of anger, embarrassment, and disappointment that he'd had up since seeing her at the club. A wall that was unsteady and, more importantly, unwanted. Truthfully, his pride was really the only reason the wall was up in the first place. Pride and stubbornness.

As shocked as he was, he knew that if Deahnna was on that stage, she was on there because she had to be. He knew her. Just as he was sure that she knew him. He knew her spirit, her character. Without even having to listen to her explanation, he knew that stripping was something she just had to do.

But still he avoided her.

It was stupid. Childish. A waste of time. And he knew it. He also knew that, at some point, he was going to return her call, and things would go back to being normal between them. Sure, they'd have to discuss the matter of removing her clothes for other men, but they'd get that matter resolved. Of that Jawan had no doubt, because he and Deahnna were meant to be together. He knew it now, just as he'd known it the first time they'd met. The stars had been aligned that evening at the dance, and the big bang had occurred.

Jawan blew his nose. The head cold he'd caught was kicking his ass. He'd stayed home from school the past two days, but he could have gone in despite the sinus pressure and the runny nose. But going to school meant that he'd have to look at Brian. And looking at Brian would only have made his wall come down sooner.

Brian.

He couldn't help but wonder if the teen knew what his mother did part-time. But even as he did wonder, he was certain that he didn't. Deahnna would never admit her sacrifice to him, and if he did know, as overprotective as he was about her, he wouldn't allow a man to look at his mother that way.

Jawan blew his nose again, and then threw the used tissue into the garbage can beside the computer desk. As he did, Grady, who'd been sitting at his feet, meowed.

He looked down at his furry companion. "Yeah, yeah. I'll call."

Grady meowed. Sounded as though he said, "Now."

Jawan shook his head. "No. Not today. I just need one more day to be an idiot. Tomorrow I'll wise up."

Grady meowed again. Something along the lines of "You better."

Jawan nodded. "Yeah, Grady-Grade. I promise."

Accepting his answer, Grady rubbed up against his leg and purred.

Jawan bent down and caressed him behind his ears. "Yeah," he said, smiling. "I miss her too."

31

"You niggas ready to do this shit?"

Brian took a deep breath as his heart jack-hammered beneath his chest. The moment he'd wanted to come and go so quickly had finally arrived, and he dreaded it.

He thought about Carla, who he'd promised to go back to later that night. She'd thrown up once and dry heaved in the time that he'd been with her after school. Her morning sickness occurred in the late afternoon, which was actually a good thing, because her mother wasn't around. But soon she would be. And not only that, but soon Carla would begin to show. They had to break the news definitely much sooner than later. They talked about that when he'd been there. That and a few other things.

What they would do before the baby came.

Where they would live.

How they would support raising a child while going to school.

Lastly, when they would get married.

Married.

Brian was as unready for that as he was being a father, but just as Carla didn't believe in having an abortion, she believed just as strongly about being married before the baby arrived.

Brian took another full breath as Tyrel waited for him and Will to answer.

Was he ready?

He exhaled at a snail's pace, his heart thumping, almost making his upper body shake with each beat.

Was he ready?

He flared his nostrils. He wasn't ready for shit.

"Let's do this shit," Will said, his tone jazzed.

Brian looked at him and thought about their last hit at the Laundromat. Will had been jazzed then, too. That dire feeling came over Brian. The feeling of impending disaster.

Back out, he thought. *Goddammit, just back out.*

Brian nodded and said, "Yeah."

Tyrel gave a short nod, and then reached into a small black book bag and pulled out the three .45s they'd used before. He handed one to Will. "Don't be usin' any names, nigga," he said.

Will nodded. "I'm good, son."

"Yeah, you better be, nigga," Tyrel said, his tone laced with warning. He turned to Brian and held out a .45 for him to take.

Brian looked at the gun and then shook his head. "I'm good."

Tyrel squinted his eyes—the only thing that could be seen through his ski mask. "What? Nigga, you better take this shit."

Brian looked at him, his gaze unflinching, and said again, "I'm good." He'd had a hard enough time dealing with what they were about to do to Old Man Blackwell. The last thing he would do was carry a gun.

Tyrel glared at Brian, while Brian stared back. Tension was as thick between them as the wool ski masks they wore.

Seconds passed before Will said, "Yo, come on, fellas. Chill wit' that shit. Ty, son, if he don't wanna use it, he don't wanna use it. You got yours. I got mine. We good."

Tyrel's eyes remained on Brian as he asked, "You sure you down for this, son? You sure you ain't gonna bitch out?"

"I'm here," Brian said, wanting to turn and run away. "I ain't bitchin' out on shit. But I'm not usin' the piece."

Tyrel looked at him.

Brian looked at Tyrel.

Seconds passed.

Then Tyrel nodded, slid Brian's .45 back in his bag, and said, "Whatever, nigga. Just keep your fuckin' eyes and ears open."

Brian gave a nod. "I got it," he said.

"You better, son."

Brian took a breath again, then lowered his ski mask over his face.

Tyrel looked at his watch, then peeked from the alley across the street they'd been hiding in. "A'ight. That nigga, Rich, is pulling the shades down. Let's do it."

Without waiting, Tyrel moved and ran across the street. Will and Brian were on his heels seconds later.

Tyrel shouldered the entrance door open just as Rich made a move to lock it, causing the door to barrel into Rich, knocking him down. Before he could think to react, Tyrel pistol-whipped Rich two times in the face, knocking him unconscious, and then grabbed him by his shirt collar and began to drag him behind the counter. "Go and get Blackwell," he said, looking at Will.

Without hesitation, Will ran behind the counter and disappeared into a back room.

Tyrel looked at Brian. "Hit the lights and watch the door, son!"

Brian took a momentary glance at Rich, who lay bleeding from his nose and mouth, and then did as instructed as Tyrel ran to the back, turned off the lights, and locked the door. From the back he heard Will yell out.

"Get your fuckin' hands up!"

Brian hated this so much. He was glad everything was happening in the back where he couldn't see.

"What the hell?" Old Man Blackwell said.

"Shut the fuck up, nigga!" Will yelled. "Or I will pull this fuckin' trigger."

"The money, old man!" Tyrel yelled. "Get that shit now!"

Brian heard Blackwell grunt out. He had no doubt he'd been hit. He gritted his teeth and kept watch outside. His heart galloped. His skin was hot and itching beneath the wool.

It was supposed to be as easy as one, two, three.

"The . . . the money's up front," Blackwell said. "I . . . I haven't removed it yet."

"Get that shit, nigga!" Tyrel yelled.

Brian looked up and down the street as he hid behind the curtained window. Seconds later, Old Man Blackwell stumbled forward from the back with Tyrel and Will in tow.

Brian looked at Blackwell, at the fear in his eyes. God, he hated this.

"My God," Blackwell said, looking down at Rich. "Is he . . ."

Tyrel said, "No. But you will be if you don't do what the fuck you're supposed to do. Now, get that fuckin' money."

He shoved Blackwell in the back, sending him crashing against the counter with the registers.

"Please," Blackwell pleaded. "Please don't do this."

"Shut the fuck up!" Tyrel yelled, hitting him in his back. "Now open that shit!"

Will, who'd been standing to the side, laughed.

Brian took a look outside. Blackwell's spot was where a gas station once stood. Luckily for them, no one was close enough to notice anything.

Brian took a look over his shoulder at Old Man Blackwell. *Please*, he thought. *Just do what they say and do it fast*. In that instant, the store's owner locked eyes with him, and, although he had a mask covering his face, Brian was almost positive that Blackwell knew who he was. Brian looked away quickly.

"Hurry up, old man!" Tyrel ordered.

Brian heard Blackwell at the register, hitting buttons. He prayed for everything to be over soon.

Buttons were hit.

The register dinged as the cash drawer opened.

"Shove the money in here, nigga!" Tyrel demanded. A few seconds later, he said, "Now the other one!"

Just as before, buttons were hit and the second register dinged open.

Soon, Brian thought. It would be over soon.

He looked up and down the block.

Then looked over his shoulder and saw something that made him yell, "No!"

From somewhere beneath the counter, Old Man Blackwell had removed a concealed pistol.

Within a span of seconds, Brian watched in slow motion as Blackwell pointed the weapon at Tyrel's head and pulled the trigger. No sound escaped from Tyrel as he fell back to the ground.

Will screamed out, pointed his .45 at Blackwell, and fired.

Blackwell gasped, fell back against the counter, and as he was falling, managed to raise his arm and fire off one shot at Will.

Brian, yelled "No!" again as Will fell back against the wall, blood pouring from his neck, while his .45 dropped from his hand.

Brian ran around the counter and stopped just short of the blood pooling from his boys and from Old Man Blackwell. "No!" he screamed again.

Will, slumped against the wall, looked up at him with his hand clamped over his neck, doing little to stop the blood flow. Brian shook his head as Will looked at him with terror and fear in his eyes. "B . . . B . . ." he stuttered, trying to speak, but unable to.

Brian shook his head again.

Will tried in vain to utter something else again, and then his hand fell from his neck as his last breath floated away.

"Will! No!" Brian yelled.

He looked over to Tyrel, who lay flat on his back, blood pooling from beneath his head. He looked to Blackwell. He was bleeding from his chest, coughing and spitting blood.

Brian put his hand behind his neck and squeezed as the room spun around him. Tyrel said this was supposed to be easy, simple. This wasn't supposed to happen. Yet, as Brian stood still, staring at blood and death, he'd known all along that this would happen.

His boys were dead. His niggas, his brothers.

He shook his head again, then removed the mask, exposing his face to Blackwell. "I . . . I'm sorry," he whispered. "Shit, I'm s . . . sorry."

Brian wiped tears away with his gloved hands as he heard sirens in the distance.

Blackwell coughed, spit blood, coughed again, and in a faint whisper said, "G . . . go."

Brian closed his eyes a bit, and looked with confusion in his eyes at the man he'd always respected. "What?"

Blackwell coughed again. "Go get . . . tape at de . . . desk."

Brian shook his head as the wailing from the sirens grew louder. "I can't go," he said. "I can't."

Blackwell coughed. "Get out n . . . now!"

Brian shook his head. Gritted his teeth. Tears fell hard, fast. He looked over at Will, then at Tyrel. His boys were gone. It didn't seem real.

Blackwell coughed once more. "B . . . Brian, go now!"

The sirens wail grew louder.

Brian looked at Blackwell. “I’m sorry,” he said. Then, making sure to avoid the blood, he stepped past his boys and Blackwell, and ran through the back room to the exit heading out to the back. But before he did, he made sure to follow Blackwell’s instructions, and grabbed the security tape from the VCR in the back.

32

Brian ran, his feet taking him where only they knew the destination. Will and Tyrel were dead. Old Man Blackwell, he was on his way.

Brian ran, blinded by tears, fear, and disbelief, down the block, away from the red and blue spiraling lights. Away from his boys.

He didn't want to believe it. Not his boys. They couldn't be dead. He struggled to stifle a scream as he ran. His boys, his brothas, his niggas.

Brian ran. He saw nothing but the sight of his lifelong friends on the ground lying in a pool of their own blood. He heard nothing but the crack of gunfire and the shrill of his own scream. He felt nothing but . . . emptiness.

He ran.

And ran.

Until his lungs demanded that he stop and take in air.

He stopped, leaned against the brick wall of a building, and took in several deep breaths of air. He was four blocks away now from the disaster that had taken place, but he was as on edge, as though he were still inside. His heartbeat refused to slow down, refused to try to stop beating its way through his chest. He felt like rubber, his hands shook. He breathed in and out. Deep, deep breaths as tears fell from the corners of his eyes.

"Damn," he whispered, slamming his head back against the wall. "Damn."

He looked up to the starless nighttime sky and prayed for the nightmare he was living to be over. *Be a dream*, he thought. *A horrible fucking dream*. He closed his eyes, and prayed that when he opened them, he'd be back at Will's sitting on his couch with Will on his right and Tyrel on his left, playing Xbox 360. Of course he knew that wouldn't be the case, and so when he opened them, he could only let out a breath.

A police siren wailed suddenly and his heart leapt into his throat. He flattened himself against the wall, unable to move.

They found me. They found me.

He couldn't breathe as one of New York's finest sped by in an unmarked car on the street in front of him, its single light flashing red, its siren wailing, and headed in the direction he'd just come from. Only when the car was out of sight did Brian allow himself to breathe and to move.

He needed to get off of the street. But where could he go? Not home. He'd held his emotions down before, but put now in front of his mother he would surely break down. So where? He needed a safe place to think, to breathe, to break down, and then pull himself back together.

Brian looked up at the sky, prayed that Will and Tyrel were somewhere up there amid the darkness, and then pushed away from the wall and ran to the safest place he could think of.

Two and a half hours later, he lay in Carla's arms, staring up at her ceiling while she slept. He'd spent a little over an hour telling her all about the three-man cartel he'd been a part of, and then telling about what had gone down hours earlier.

Carla, who hadn't known about any of the activities he'd done with Will and Tyrel, laid into him. How could he do this? What had he been thinking? He was an idiot.

An asshole. On and on she went, and then in Spanish, sounding far more pissed off. Brian took it all without a word because she'd been right with everything she'd said. He was an immature, irresponsible, disrespectful idiot. He was pitiful, weak. After Carla finished ripping him a new one and telling him how disappointed she was in him, she helped him come up with an alibi for when the cops came knocking on his door, which he knew they would.

Brian stared up at the ceiling, reliving moments he knew he would never forget. He closed his fists. If he could only go back, he thought. But of course he couldn't. The cards had been dealt and turned over. There was no giving back to the dealer the hand he'd been given. He unclenched his fists.

His boys.

Old Man Blackwell.

He took a slow breath. Old Man Blackwell. He'd told him to take the tape, told him to leave. Why? It was a question he'd never have an answer for.

Brian took another slow, deep breath. He'd had no gun in his hand, and he hadn't pulled any triggers, but Old Man Blackwell's blood was on his hands just as surely as if he'd been holding the piece of steel with his finger curled around the trigger. That fact hurt his heart almost as though he'd taken a bullet point blank. He closed his eyes while tears welled once more and leaked from the corners.

33

Deahnna rolled over onto her side and looked at her alarm clock. It was nine o'clock in the morning. She should have been up since six, cleaning and dusting. Her Saturday morning ritual. But she didn't feel like cleaning or dusting. She didn't feel like doing much of anything.

Three days had now passed since she'd last seen Jawan. More, if you consider the fact that their last time together had been one she wanted to forget.

Three days.

Seventy-two hours of loneliness.

She stared at the time displayed. Watched one, then two minutes click by. Minutes that seemed like hours. She looked from the clock to her cell phone sitting beside it. It hadn't rung in the middle of the night. It hadn't chimed, letting her know that a message was waiting for her to listen to. That meant Jawan hadn't called. She frowned. She wanted to pick it up and call him again, but what was the use?

She opened her mouth, took a deep breath, and blew it out as her eyes threatened to well. She shook her head and pressed her palms against her eyes. *No,* she thought. *No more.* She wasn't going to cry anymore. She'd made the bed and she would have to lie in it. Even if she wasn't completely in the wrong.

She didn't want to, but she swung her feet off of the bed, slid into her slippers, and stood up. Three days had passed and he hadn't called. Surely he'd gotten her messages. She didn't want to, but she had no choice: she had to move on. Move on and continue to survive, knowing and accepting that love and happiness just wasn't in the deck she'd been given when she was born.

She took a final glance at her phone, and then slid on her robe and went into the bathroom to brush her teeth. As she did, there was a knock on the front door. Her heartbeat quickened. Jawan? Could it be? Her toothbrush in her mouth, she called out to her son. "Brian, can you get the door?"

She finished brushing, then washed out her mouth, and quickly ran water over her face and through her hair. She didn't have time to shower, but at least she could look presentable.

Knocking came from the door again. Harder. More insistent.

She dried her face, did the best she could to spruce up her hair, and then went to Brian's bedroom door and pushed it open as the knocking continued. "Brian." She paused. His room was empty. His bed still made up from the day before. "Dammit," she whispered.

She shook her head, promised to have a very serious, no-nonsense heart–to-heart with her son about being under her roof and having to follow her rules, and then rushed to the front door.

"Coming!" she yelled out, tightening the sash on her robe.

She took a look through the peephole and her heart fell to the pit of her stomach. On the other side of the door, dressed in blue uniforms, with their hats on their heads, were two police officers. Deahnna felt a shiver come over her. Brian wasn't in his room and hadn't been all night. Now the police were at her door at nine o'clock in the morning. "Oh, God," she whispered.

She opened the door slightly "Yes, can I help you?"

One of the officers, the taller of the two, with dark

brown skin, a clean-shaven face, and deep-set dark brown eyes smiled and said, "Hello. Are you Brian Moore's mother?"

Deahnna nodded. "I am."

"I'm Officer Cribbs. This is my partner, Officer Lomax."

Deahnna looked at Officer Lomax, a shorter, stockier man with a whisper of a goatee and a scowl on his face, and then looked back to Officer Cribbs. "Can I help you?"

"We're looking for your son, Brian."

"Brian? Is he in some sort of trouble?"

Officer Cribbs shook his head. "We just have some questions that we'd like to ask him."

"Questions about what?"

"We'd really rather talk with Brian before we discuss the nature of our visit."

Deahnna looked at them skeptically. "Well, I'm sorry, officer, but my son is—"

"Mom?"

Deahnna looked past the officer's shoulders, down to see Brian approaching. "Brian," she said, her tone sharp.

The officers turned as Brian stood still.

"Wh . . . what's up, Mom?"

"Are you Brian Moore?" Officer Cribbs asked as his partner looked on.

Brian nodded. "Yeah."

"I'm Officer Cribbs. This is Officer Lomax. We'd like to ask you a couple of questions."

Brian looked at his mother, and, in that moment, Deahnna could see in his eyes that something had happened. She gave him a nod.

Brian looked at Officer Cribbs. "OK."

Officer Cribbs turned back to Deahnna. "May we come inside?"

Deahnna opened the door. “Come in.”

Both officers followed Brian inside. Deahnna directed them to the living room, where everyone sat down: the two officers on the sofa, Brian on the loveseat, Deahnna on the loveseat’s arm beside her son.

Officer Cribbs pulled out a notepad and looked at Brian. “Are you now just getting home?”

Brian nodded. “Yeah.”

“From where?”

“My girlfriend’s place.”

Deahnna looked down at her son, who kept his head low.

“Your girlfriend’s name?”

“Carla.”

“Her last name?”

“Quinones.”

“And her address.”

Brian gave it.

“Were you there between eleven-thirty and twelve last night?”

Brian nodded. “Yeah. I was there all night.”

“Excuse me?” Deahnna said. “Her parents allowed this?”

Brian looked up at his mother. “Her mother didn’t know. I snuck in.”

“What? Brian, goddammit . . .”

Officer Cribbs cleared his throat. “Brian, are you friends with Will Barber and Tyrel Gardner?”

Deahnna stared hard at her son. If the cop mentioned Will or Tyrel’s name, that meant that there was trouble. She watched Brian closely as he let a few seconds go by before he said in a softer tone, “Yeah. They’re my . . . my best friends.”

“Did you see them last night?”

Brian intertwined his fingers. “I . . . I mean, we played the 360 for a while after school, and then I left to go and see Carla.”

"What time was that?" Cribbs asked after scribbling down some notes.

"I left Will's place around five."

"And you stayed with Ms. Quinones all night?"

Brian nodded, then shrugged. "Well, not then. I hung with her for a little and then left before her mom got home."

"And where did you go?"

"I came home."

A chill came over Deahnna as she forced herself to not look down at Brian. She'd gotten home at five-thirty and had gone to bed at eleven-thirty. Brian had never come home. Too depressed over Jawan ignoring her, she'd never bother trying to call Brian to see where he was, and unlike any other time, she never bothered waiting up.

Officer Cribbs looked at her. "Were you home around that time, Ms. Moore?"

She nodded. "Yes."

"And you saw Brian come home."

"Yes. I did."

"And you never saw him leave?"

She looked down at Brian who kept his sights on the floor. "No," she said. "I didn't."

Officer Cribbs nodded, scribbled in his pad, and then looked at Brian. "Brian, Will and Tyrel were both killed last night."

Brian looked up. "Wh . . . what?"

Deahnna put her hand over her mouth. "My God," she whispered.

"It was a botched robbery attempt."

Brian shook his head. "No way," he said, tears falling from his eyes. "You're . . . you're lying."

Officer Cribbs frowned. "I'm afraid not."

"They . . . they can't be dead," Brian said, his voice cracking. "Not my boys."

Deahnna leaned over and wrapped her arms around her son and held him tightly. "I'm so sorry," she whispered, kissing him on the top of his head. She looked at Officer Cribbs. "Is my son in some sort of trouble, Officer?"

"Not unless he knew about what his friends had planned. Did you know they were planning anything, Brian?"

Brian shook his head. "N . . . no."

Officer Cribbs looked at his partner, who gave a subtle shake of his head. Cribbs looked back to Deahnna. "No, Ms. Moore. We got Brian's name after questioning people who knew Will and Tyrel. We were told about how close they were. We just wanted to come and talk to him. We'll corroborate his alibi with Ms. Quinones."

"And then?"

"And then if everything checks out, that will be it."

Deahnna nodded. "How did Will and Tyrel die?" she asked, rubbing Brian's shoulders as he sobbed.

"They were shot by the establishment's owner, who was also shot."

"My God," she whispered. "Did . . . did he or she die as well?"

Officer Cribbs shook his head. "No. He took a bullet to his chest, but, fortunately for him, he survived. He's in stable condition right now. We were actually able to question him, and he did confirm that he'd only been accosted by two people."

"So why did you come here?"

"Just wanted to dot all of the Is and cross all of the Ts."

Deahnna nodded.

Both officers stood up. "Thank you both for your time," Cribbs said. "Brian, sorry about your friends. Lucky for you that you weren't hanging with them last night." Cribbs turned, looked at his silent partner, and gave a head motion toward the door.

Deahnna kissed her son on his head again, left him on the loveseat, and escorted the officers to the door.

"We'll speak with Ms. Quinones," Cribbs said, stepping out of the apartment. "But again, as long as their stories gel, we won't be bothering your son again."

Deahnna gave the officer a half smile. "Thank you."

Cribbs turned to leave and then stopped and turned back around. He took a look toward Brian, and then looked at Deahnna. "Ms. Moore," he said, his eyes serious, intense. "Your son is a very lucky young man," he said. "I hope he understands that."

She looked at the officer, who looked back at her with an unflinching gaze. "I do," she said.

Officer Cribbs gave her a nod, and then turned and left.

Deahnna closed the door, dropped her chin to her chest, and let out the breath she hadn't yet exhaled. She shook her head, and then turned and went back to her son.

Brian looked up at her, his eyes red as tears ran furiously. "I'm sorry, Mom," he said, his voice barely audible. "I . . . I'm sorry."

Deahnna took him in her arms, and let him bury his head into her. She stroked the top of his head and cried her own tears. "Oh, Brian."

34

Her son was lucky and he was about to become a father. Under normal circumstances, Deahnna would have flipped out. He was only seventeen. Didn't he know better than to be out there having unprotected sex? He had so much promise ahead of him. Didn't he realize how being a teenage parent would affect him, his life, his plans? Wasn't he smarter that that? Hadn't she raised him with more sense?

Under normal circumstances, that would have been her reaction. Under normal circumstances, she would have said those things and a whole lot more.

But the circumstances weren't normal because he'd been lucky. So very, very lucky.

Old Man Blackwell had survived. A man she'd known since she was a teenager herself. A man who'd been there for her as he had been for many others, offering an ear, advice, counsel, and sometimes money. He was known and respected by all, because he treated everyone as though they mattered.

Deahnna still couldn't believe that her son had a hand in his getting hurt. He hadn't told her the details, and, honestly, she didn't want to know them, but his lies to the police and his very sincere, tearful apology had been enough to let her know that not only did he know what was going on, but that he was a part of it, because she knew he would do as his friends had done, as much as she'd tried and failed to convince him not to in the past.

But he was lucky. Sadly, Will and Tyrel were dead. Old Man Blackwell had survived. And now Brian was going to be a father.

Deahnna watched Brian sleeping in his bed. After Officer Cribbs and his partner left, Brian shed what seemed to be an endless stream of tears as he apologized without specifics for what had happened, and then told her about the dilemma he and his girlfriend, Carla, faced. Again, under different circumstances, her reaction to the news would have been one that would have most likely pushed him away. But he was at home, sleeping in his bed, instead of in a pine box.

Teenage father or not, his time hadn't come yet. His destiny hadn't been fulfilled.

She smiled. It had been a long time since she'd tucked her angel in. She said a silent prayer, thanking God for the opportunity to do that, and then closed his bedroom door softly. Later that day, she and Brian were going to go over to Carla's to talk to both Carla and her mother. Deahnna could only imagine what Carla's mother must be feeling or thinking with her little girl being pregnant. Unlike Deahnna, Carla's mother had no other special circumstances to lessen the blow from the surprising news.

Deahnna shook her head and went into the kitchen to put on some water to boil. Although she'd had one hell of a kick-start to her day, she still needed her morning cup of tea.

As she turned the fire on beneath the kettle, her cell phone rang. She went to her room to grab her phone. Her mind occupied by the activities from the morning, she hadn't given any thought about who could have been calling, so when she saw Jawan's name on the screen, she paused.

He was calling.

Deahnna felt a hot flush come over her.

He was calling.

She whispered, “Thank you,” and then, after a deep breath and a slow exhale, she answered.

35

He'd promised both Grady and himself that he would stop being a fool. He loved her. He needed her. Needed to hear her, see her, feel her, hold her. He needed to be with her again, and forever, if she'd have him. He wanted to call when he'd first woken up, but that had been at five in the morning, since he'd been unable to sleep. She was all he could think about. All he could dream about. No more sitting on the beach with Janet Jackson. No more nightmares about his ex, Kim. It was all about Deahnna Moore. And an appropriate hour had finally and mercifully arrived for him to make his call.

So he did.

With a thumping heartbeat.

"Hello?"

He smiled. God, he loved the sound of her voice. Like honey. He said, "Hey."

She said, "Hi."

Silence interrupted them for a second or two before he asked, "How have you been?"

"I . . . I've been . . ." Deahnna paused. "I've been miserable," she said honestly.

Jawan sucked his lips in. "So have I," he said.

"Jawan, I'm sorry."

"Shh," he said, cutting her off. "Don't apologize."

"But—"

"No buts, Deahnna. We have some things to talk about, but an apology won't be part of the conversation. It's not needed or wanted. OK?"

Deahnna was silent for a moment before she said, “OK.”

“I’ve missed you, Deahnna.”

“I’ve missed you too.”

Jawan smiled, and pet his furry companion, who was sitting beside him on his couch. “Grady missed you too.”

Deahnna laughed. “Tell Grady I’ve been worried about him.”

“You should probably come and tell him that face-to-face. He might not believe it coming from me.”

“Tell you what: why don’t you bring him here and I’ll tell him.”

Jawan raised an eyebrow. “Bring him there?”

“Yes.”

“And what about Brian?”

Deahnna frowned. “There’s a lot going on where Brian’s concerned. You being here is the least of his worries.”

“Is he all right?”

“He has some . . . growing pains he has to endure. Actually, I think it would be very good if you came by tomorrow to have a heart-to-heart with him, while I have my own with Grady.”

“Tomorrow? I was hoping to see you today,” he said, slightly disappointed.

“Brian and I have some things we have to deal with today. I’ll tell you all about them tomorrow. I promise.”

“OK.”

“I’m glad you called,” Deahnna said.

Jawan tapped Grady lightly on the top of his head. Grady looked up at him and purred. “So am I,” he said, rubbing Grady’s ear. “So am I.”

Epilogue

8 months later

Brian couldn't believe it.

He was a father.

He held his son, Israel, in his arms, and couldn't help it—he cried. His son. His little man.

For eight months his emotions had gone from fear, to excitement, to nervous anticipation, and then back to fear, to excitement, to nervousness. He was going to be a father. Something he'd never had. What was he supposed to do? How was he supposed to be? What were the rules? For eight months the fear, the doubt, the uncertainty swirled in his mind. He took parenting preparation classes with Carla. He read books. He sought advice from his mom and from Carla's mom, but nothing had helped to relieve the tension.

But now, holding Israel in his arms for the first time, that anxiety, that trepidation, that doubt that he'd been riddled with was gone. Although the unknown still remained, the feeling of not knowing what to do or how to do it wasn't there. Perhaps it was a little naive of him to think so, but standing with his five-pound, six-ounce, twenty-three-inch bundle with a full head of hair, in his arms, he felt nothing but calm. He was a father, and he was sure that he was going to be the best damn father he could be.

Israel Eric Moore would never have to worry about ever having a life without his father there to guide and protect him. This Brian promised his son as he held him gently but tightly at the same time.

"He's precious, just like you were."

Brian looked up. His mother was standing in the doorway, watching him with a smile and tears of her own. Beside her was Mr. White. Well, Jawan, as he insisted on being called now that he was his stepfather.

Brian looked at both of them and smiled. Life had changed dramatically in the eight months since everything had happened on that fateful night at Old Man Blackwell's.

Blackwell, who'd recovered completely, had decided to retire, and passed the business on to Rich, who would forever be a drug addict, but who also never had the desire to walk down the dark road again. Brian had never gotten to ask Blackwell why he'd let him go. He'd never had the nerve to go and see him. Maybe one day he would try to find him and get the answer. Maybe.

He'd attended the funerals for both Will and Tyrel. That had been hard. He'd never imagined ever having to say a final good-bye to his best friends. For a few weeks, he struggled with feelings of guilt. The plan had never been his, nor had it been one he'd wanted to be part of, but he'd survived when they hadn't. It was hard for him to not feel pangs of guilt for that. But eventually he overcame those feelings and moved on, thanks to the support and patience from his mother, Jawan, and Carla.

Speaking of his mother and now stepfather.

Three months after everything happened, they moved in together. Well, Brian and his mother moved in with Jawan. It was awkward for Brian at first. After all, Jawan was still his teacher, and he hadn't forgotten how Jawan had lied to his face. But the ill and awkward feelings quickly disappeared as Brian watched the smile on his mother's face grow wider with each passing day. Jawan loved his mother and didn't hesitate to display his affection for her, something his mother deserved.

He also didn't hold back on the fact that he cared for Brian and wanted nothing but the best for him. It was weird getting that attention from a man, since that was something he'd never received before, but with time, the weird feeling went away as it just became the norm. As a matter of fact, his life just felt as though Jawan had always been a part of it. So when they married at the courthouse two months after moving in together, it had been no big deal.

Brian rocked his son gently, and accepted a kiss from his mother as she took Israel out of his arms, kissed, and "ooh'd" over him, and then went to Carla, who lay in the hospital bed with her mother sitting beside her, and gave them both kisses and hugs.

"You did good, Brian," Jawan said, giving him a one-armed hug.

Brian smiled. "Yeah," he said.

"You did good with her, too," Jawan said, his voice softer, his head motioning in Carla's direction.

Brian looked at Carla and smiled. They hadn't gotten married as she'd wanted to before Israel was born, but not because he didn't want to. Truth was, Brian wanted very much to make Carla his wife, as he'd fallen deeper in love with her as they went through the strains of pregnancy. She had his back and he would always remember and respect that. He'd always felt that she was special, but the more they grew together, the more he realized just how rare of a gem she was.

He wanted to marry her, but hadn't only because his mother, Jawan, and Carla's mother persuaded them to wait. Marriage was an important step, and while no one doubted what they felt for one another, they just wanted them to wait at least until they graduated from high school.

Brian had no problem with that, because he knew in his heart that he and Carla would be just fine, and that marriage would simply be a matter of time. They had a lot of challenges ahead of them. High school to graduate from. College to attend. A life to build. But Brian had no doubt they would conquer each and every obstacle in their path.

He nodded as he watched Carla holding their son, while the grandmothers gushed. “Yeah,” he said proudly. “I did.”

End

ORDER FORM
URBAN BOOKS, LLC
78 E. Industry Ct
Deer Park, NY 11729

Name: (please print):____

Address: ____

City/State: ____

Zip: ____

QTY	TITLES	PRICE
	16 ½ On The Block	$14.95
	16 On The Block	$14.95
	Betrayal	$14.95
	Both Sides Of The Fence	$14.95
	Cheesecake And Teardrops	$14.95
	Denim Diaries	$14.95
	Happily Ever Now	$14.95
	Hell Has No Fury	$14.95
	If It Isn't love	$14.95
	Last Breath	$14.95
	Loving Dasia	$14.95
	Say It Ain't So	$14.95

Shipping and handling-add $3.50 for 1st book, then $1.75 for each additional book.

Please send a check payable to:

Urban Books, LLC

Please allow 4-6 weeks for delivery

ORDER FORM
URBAN BOOKS, LLC
78 E. Industry Ct
Deer Park, NY 11729

Name: (please print):____________________________________

Address: ____________________________________

City/State: ____________________________________

Zip: ____________________________________

QTY	TITLES	PRICE
	The Cartel	$14.95
	The Cartel 2	$14.95
	The Dopeman's Wife	$14.95
	The Prada Plan	$14.95
	Gunz And Roses	$14.95
	Snow White	$14.95
	A Pimp's Life	$14.95
	Hush	$14.95
	Little Black Girl Lost 1	$14.95
	Little Black Girl Lost 2	$14.95
	Little Black Girl Lost 3	$14.95
	Little Black Girl Lost 4	$14.95

Shipping and handling-add $3.50 for 1st book, then $1.75 for each additional book.
Please send a check payable to:
Urban Books, LLC
Please allow 4-6 weeks for delivery

ORDER FORM
URBAN BOOKS, LLC
78 E. Industry Ct
Deer Park, NY 11729

Name: (please print):________________________________

Address: ________________________________

City/State: ________________________________

Zip: ________________________________

QTY	TITLES	PRICE
	A Man's Worth	$14.95
	Abundant Rain	$14.95
	Battle Of Jericho	$14.95
	By The Grace Of God	$14.95
	Dance Into Destiny	$14.95
	Divorcing The Devil	$14.95
	Forsaken	$14.95
	Grace And Mercy	$14.95
	Guilty Of Love	$14.95
	His Woman, His Wife, His Widow	$14.95
	Illusions	$14.95
	The LoveChild	$14.95

Shipping and handling-add $3.50 for 1st book, then $1.75 for each additional book.
Please send a check payable to:
Urban Books, LLC
Please allow 4-6 weeks for delivery

ORDER FORM
URBAN BOOKS, LLC
78 E. Industry Ct
Deer Park, NY 11729

Name: (please print):_______________________________

Address: _______________________________

City/State: _______________________________

Zip: _______________________________

QTY	TITLES	PRICE

Shipping and handling-add $3.50 for 1st book, then $1.75 for each additional book.

Please send a check payable to:

Urban Books, LLC

Please allow 4-6 weeks for delivery